Freshman Flash

by
Mike Boushell

Royal Fireworks Press

Unionville, New York

Royal Fireworks Press
First Ave, PO Box 399
Unionville, NY 10988
(845) 726-4444
FAX: (845) 726-3824
email: rfpress@frontiernet.net

ISBN: 0-88092-600-7

Printed in the United States of America on recycled paper using
vegetable-based inks by the Royal Fireworks Printing Company of
Unionville, New York.

CHAPTER 1

Run Over

Danny Cannon was third in the tackling line, and it was clear that he'd be going against Big Dog Perez, one of the toughest guys on the varsity. Danny was only a ninth grader, and he was feeling more and more nervous as his turn grew closer.

The next two players squared off and waited for the coach's signal. "Ready. Go!" shouted Coach Cook.

Tim Kern and Brian Hanlon smashed together and went down in a pile of arms and legs. Coach Wilson, the defensive linebacker coach, bellowed his approval. "Way to hit," he yelled.

Barry Edwards, a six foot, two-hundred-pound tackle, was next man in the tackling line. Skeeter Simms, a quick but undersized sophomore halfback was to be the next ball carrier.

Edwards turned to Danny. "Switch with me," he said. "He's more your size." For an instant Danny felt relief wash over him. Then, because of what he later realized was a combination of pride and pure insanity, he said, "Thanks, but I want the Big Dog."

"What's going on over there?" demanded Coach Wilson.

"I was just trying to trade match-ups with this freshman, Coach," said Edwards.

"So what's the problem?"

1

"He doesn't want to switch."

"Why not?"

"He says he wants the Big Dog." Barry Edwards was grinning as he spoke.

"Tell him he's got me," sneered Big Dog Perez.

Danny swallowed hard, braced himself, and waited for the coach's signal. Coach Cook waited a second to allow both boys a chance to get themselves set. "Ready. Go!" he yelled.

Big Dog Perez charged straight at Danny. He had no intention of wasting a fancy move on the freshman. His plan wasn't just to go by him; it was to hurt him. If he could humiliate him in the process, so much the better.

Danny dug in, bracing himself for the impact. He stepped in front of Perez, aiming his shoulder for the ball carrier's thighs. He had been through similar tackling drills dozens of times at the junior high level. In the seventh and eighth grades, he had earned the reputation of being a deadly tackler. He had always followed the advice of his coaches, and had learned to bull his neck and keep his head up. He kept his eyes focused on the Big Dog's waist. He did everything right. The result should have been a picture perfect tackle. Instead, Danny felt a sharp pain as the tough senior lowered his shoulder and banged him to the ground. The cocky upperclassman went into an exaggerated high-step as he left Danny empty-armed in his dust. "What you doin' chewin' that dirt, chump?" he asked Danny, grinning. "I thought you say you want a shot at the Big Dog."

Danny jumped to his feet. Pain raced through his right shoulder, but it was nothing compared to the embarrassment that flooded over him. Danny had never felt so humiliated on a football field.

"Next," yelled Coach Wilson.

Half of Danny wanted to try again, and he was just getting up the nerve to ask for another try when the coach instructed Barry Edwards to line up against the Big Dog. Danny moved slowly towards the back of the line. Edwards was a sturdy lineman, not a starter, but a solid varsity sub. He buckled up his chinstrap and awaited the coach's signal to fire out.

When Coach Cook yelled, "Go," Edwards charged directly at the Big Dog. This time Perez side-stepped, eluded Edwards' grasping hands, and once more taunted a would-be tackler.

"Can't nobody tackle the Big Dog. He too slippery. He too quick. He just like Barry Sanders in his prime."

Half amused and half impressed, Coach Wilson called up Vince Detzi, a tough starting tackle, and watched as the Big Dog spun out of his grasp and continued his cocky taunts. "Anyone else want to try?" the coach asked. "Maybe we really do have the next Barry Sanders playing for the Warriors."

"I'll give it a try," said a voice from the back of the line.

"Well, well, if it ain't Bo James his own self," said the Big Dog. "Come on, my brother. You might as well taste the dirt too. Ain't none of you chumps can tackle the Big Dog. I thought by now you'd know that."

Bo James made no reply. He just smiled at the Big Dog. At five ten, a hundred and ninety pounds, Bo James wasn't exceptionally big, but in that five foot ten frame he packed a wallop like few fans of Rockland High football had ever witnessed. He had been All-League at both linebacker and fullback in each of his first three seasons at Rockland, a rare accomplishment, and an honor accorded very few players in the tough Pennsylvania Mountain Conference. Freshmen seldom even suited up for varsity games, never started, and certainly never made All-League. That is, unless you were Bo James, as close to a living legend as Rockland High School had ever produced, and Rockland had long been known as a football powerhouse.

Last year Bo James was named as a starting linebacker to the All-State team. In addition, he was selected to the All-State second team at the fullback position. Only Joey "Mach 2" Moore, a senior from the western part of the state, had piled up more yardage or scored more touchdowns than Bo James. There were those around the Pittsburgh area who felt that Moore was the greatest running back since Tony Dorsett. But those who had seen Bo James contended that, if the two stars ever met, Bo James would outrun, out-hit, and generally out-perform "the Pittsburgh Rocket" (a Pittsburgh newspaper had felt compelled to give "Mach 2" a second epithet).

Danny watched expectantly as Bo James faced the Big Dog. Perez was still trash talking when Coach Cook shouted, "Go!"

The word had hardly left Coach's lips when Bo James lowered his shoulder and drove it into the flashy tailback. From that point the Big Dog was in reverse, no longer in control. Arms flailing, feet lifted completely off the ground, the Big Dog was frantically searching for a spot to land. He had little time to search. Bo James unceremoniously dumped him three yards behind his starting point. Then, without a word, he stretched out his hand and helped the now quiet ball carrier to his feet.

"That, gentlemen, is how it's done," said Coach Wilson. "Any questions?"

"That don't count," said the Big Dog. "That was Bo James. He ain't human. Ain't no human tackler can tackle the Big Dog, and that a well-known fact. You had to call in your pet monster to tackle the Big Dog. Don't none of the rest of you jive turkeys think that just 'cause some alien bein' go and tackle the Big Dog that mean any of you chumps can do it, 'cause it don't. And that's no jive."

Coach Wilson and Coach Cook grinned at each other. "Agility drills!" yelled Coach Wilson, and both the ball carriers and tacklers jogged over to where the quarterbacks and receivers were practicing their pass patterns.

The next twenty minutes were Danny's least favorite part of practice: bear crawls, shoulder rolls, up-downs, and suicides. Just when he was certain his body couldn't endure another minute of agility drills, the coach lined everyone up for wind sprints, forty-yard dashes, until everyone was ready to drop. Finally, when he was too exhausted even to care, the coach yelled "Take it in boys." Then and only then was Danny sure he survived another day.

Once in the locker room, Danny stripped off his sweat-soaked jersey, tugged off his pants, peeled out of his pads, and dropped to the bench beside his locker. He sat there for a minute or two before grabbing his towel and heading for the showers. Now the only thought in his mind was to cool off. He could hardly wait to feel the cool spray. It was like some magic potion that restored the dead to life. Day after day he had staggered into the shower room, certain that he'd be too tired ever to leave. Day after day the cool water had worked its magic, quickly bringing his body back to life. Today would be no different.

The cool spray felt good on Danny's exhausted body. The August heat had taken its toll on even the best conditioned athletes. Danny had never worked so hard for so long. He began to wonder if his hard work would ever pay off.

CHAPTER 2

Danny Meets His Hero

Walking home that night, Danny kept reliving the tackling session in his mind. He was sure he had done everything exactly as Coach Bechtel had taught him back in junior high. He had squared up to the ball carrier, focused his eyes on the runner's waist (so he couldn't be easily faked out of position), kept his legs under him, and kept his head up as he had made his hit. Still, the Big Dog had shaken him off like, well, like a dog shakes off rainwater. He didn't get it. What did he do wrong?

Danny's walk home usually took him about twenty-five minutes. He lived nearly two miles away, so even moving at a brisk pace, it was more than just a short stretch of the legs, especially when those legs were dead tired from a hard football practice session.

While he was still deep in thought, a car pulled up alongside of him. Ross Tanner was driving, and Bo James was leaning out the window signaling to Danny. "Hey kid, hop in, and we'll give you a lift," the star linebacker called.

"Thanks. But I'm not supposed to take a ride with strangers," Danny began.

"Are we strangers?" the captain of the team grinned.

Danny flushed. "'Course not. But my mom might not understand."

"Suit yourself kid," said Bo James. "We just wanted to tell you that it took guts to take a crack at the Big Dog the way you did. Not many freshmen would even have tried to tackle him."

The last thing Danny had expected for missing a tackle was praise.

"Yeah," chimed in Ross Tanner. "He may have a big mouth, but he's plenty hard to tackle. I've missed him once or twice myself."

Danny saw that the upperclassman was being honest, not sarcastic. Tanner had a reputation of being plenty tough. He and Bo James were close buddies, and there were rumors that on one occasion the two of them stood back to back and took on seven bullies who were intent on making a reputation by beating up the highly publicized high school football star. Not backing away from a fight was something admired in this tough, blue-collar town.

Danny felt flattered that the two seniors even knew who he was, but he had promised his mom that he wouldn't ride with anyone she hadn't personally approved of. Still, he was sure she would have approved of Bo James and his friend. He hesitated, was about to accept, then thought better of it. "Thanks anyway you guys, but I don't live that far away."

"No sweat, kid," said Bo James. "See ya at practice tomorrow." The car pulled smoothly away and quickly accelerated out of sight.

When Danny got home, his mother was out of the house. With his hectic schedule and his mom's job, it seemed that the two of them seldom saw each other any more. Because he and his mom had been close from the time he was born, he missed the time they spent together, and he knew that she missed it as much as he did, and more.

On the kitchen table, his mom had left a note saying that she had to run some errands. It informed him that there was chili in a lidded dish in the fridge. It needed only to be warmed in the microwave. There was a salad next to it. All Danny had to do was add the salad dressing. Danny noted that his mom had remembered how much he liked hard rolls with his chili. She had drawn a little picture on the note with an arrow pointing to the breadbox. The note said, "No, I didn't forget your rolls. They're in the breadbox. Hope school and practice went well. See you in about an hour. Love, Mom." There was a smiley face and a lot of X's and O's at the bottom of the note. It was the kind of note his mom would leave. From the time he was born, the two of them were about as close as any mother and son could ever be.

Danny's mother and father had split up when Danny was still in diapers. His mom no longer spoke of his dad. Danny knew very little about what had happened between them. He did know that somehow his dad had managed to vanish, and since then had made almost no effort to stay in contact with either Danny or his mother. Once or twice a year, his mother would get a letter from his father. His mom would never let Danny know exactly what the letter said, but she'd always slowly shake her head saying, "It looks like your father's conscience must be bothering him again." Then she'd pull out his check for a hundred or, on rare occasions, two hundred dollars. This usually occurred around Christmastime or in the middle of April (just about the time of Danny's birthday). It wasn't money that could be counted on, but at least it was something. Danny's mom said that she wished she could afford to just tear up the check and send it back, but with her making as little as she did as a secretary for the school's guidance counselors, she couldn't afford that luxury.

She refused to let her pride take their food off the table or presents from under their tree. So she cashed the check and swallowed her pride. Danny resolved that one day he'd earn so much money his mom could do whatever she wanted to with those checks that she hated to cash.

Though Danny never told anyone, his dream was to play pro football. But he knew that to have any chance of ever attaining that dream, first he would have to go to college. He wanted desperately to earn an athletic scholarship to a university, for without it he was certain that his mom could not afford to send him. Danny thought about it long and hard, and he decided that, as long as the college or university had a football program, he would be willing to play for just about anyone.

Because of his dream, Danny felt he had to make the varsity this season. He realized that if he were to reach his goal, he'd need to be able to tackle plenty of running backs, some even tougher than the Big Dog. If he played

10

big-time college football he'd surely be required to tackle a back as tough as Bo James. That's why Danny was feeling so low. He was beginning to doubt his own ability, something that had never happened to him before.

Danny's mind drifted again and again to the day's events. Before today, he was been confident he could tackle anyone. He was the surest tackler on the junior high squad. He never doubted himself then, not for an instant. Now, he wasn't sure. Perhaps he wasn't as good as he thought. Perhaps Coach Bechtel had been wrong about him. Maybe he had peaked too soon and would never get any better. Danny couldn't stop worrying about how easily the Big Dog had eluded him that afternoon. He wondered if the Big Dog was really that good, or if he himself was actually not nearly as good as he had been told.

CHAPTER 3

A Face from the Past

Even as Danny began heating his supper, Nancy Cannon was fueling up her car and preparing to drive home. She was in the act of pulling the metal nozzle gas hose out of her old car's gas tank, when she noticed a man staring at her. He wasn't just looking, he was gawking, and the thought that a man would be so brazenly giving her the once-over caused her to blush. Back in high school she frequently drew flirtatious stares and appreciative comments. That was before graduation, before she attended Penn State University, met, fell in love with, and married Jeffrey Cannon.

The man she now referred to as "the greatest mistake I ever made" was then a college senior. Jeff Cannon. Tall, blond, and handsomer than any man she had ever met. It was during her freshman year in college that he swept her off her feet with his wit, good looks, and charm. These qualities, coupled with his undying promise to make her "perpetually happy," eventually convinced her to forego her college education and marry the "man of her dreams."

Her decision resulted in six months of bliss, two and a half years of heartache, and a bitter divorce that left her with a son to raise as a single parent. Despite everything he had done to ruin her life, Nancy sometimes thought of how she might feel if her ex-husband would ever come back. Whenever she permitted this fantasy to enter her mind, she chided herself for being both foolish and self-destructive, and then threw herself headlong into the rearing of her son, the only worthwhile thing to come out of her marriage.

Nancy hung up the nozzle of the gas pump, waited for the computer to print out her receipt, and prepared to leave for home. But even now, the man who had been watching her was walking towards her, apparently intent upon speaking to her. When she looked directly at him a flash of recognition flooded over her. He started to speak.

"Nancy, Nancy Evans," he began, smiling. "You're prettier than ever. What are you doing back here in Rockland?"

The voice, the smile—it all came rushing back to her. He was Steve Mitman, who had taken her, in her sophomore year, to his senior prom. She had been desperately in love with him once. Her father hadn't approved and told her that Steve was "too old, and way too serious," for a young girl like her. Eventually they stopped dating. Steve went away to school, and that was the last she heard of him. Now, here he was, telling her how pretty she still looked. But certainly he must be married. He was such "a hunk" back in high school, and he looked almost the same. Except for a few added pounds, a wrinkle or two on his brow, and much nicer clothes, Steve Mitman hadn't changed at all.

"Why, I live here," she said. "That is, my son and I live here." She wasn't quite sure why she had felt the need to throw the fact that she had a son into the conversation so soon, but she did.

"Oh, I see," he said. "You're married then?"

"Well, I was," she replied. "But I've been divorced for quite awhile now. What about you? I mean, how are you doing?"

"I'm still an old bachelor," he said. "I guess that after you the rest of them just couldn't stack up."

"I see you still know just what to say to a girl," Nancy Cannon smiled. It was the first time she had actually allowed herself to smile so openly in the company of a man in a very long time, and it felt good. Nancy was surprised that she really was beginning to feel attractive again. The two old friends talked for what must have been close to twenty minutes. It wasn't until a car honked its agitation at them that they went on their way. She had, much to her own surprise, given Steve her home phone number. He, in turn, had given her both the phone number of the hotel at which he was staying, and his home number. He explained that he had come to town to scout Bo James for the University of Michigan. Steve, it seems, was an assistant coach there. She should have guessed it. Next to Bo James, Steve Mitman was the best football player Rockland High School ever produced.

Nancy permitted her mind to drift as she drove home. It wasn't often she allowed herself to speculate on "what-ifs" or "might-have-beens", but tonight she allowed herself to indulge.   Before she knew it, she was pulling into her driveway.

Meanwhile, Danny had been following the routine he had grown accustomed to every school night for the past three years.   Once he had finished dinner, he spent between an hour and an hour and a half on his homework.   He found that except on those nights when he had to put in an extra thirty or forty minutes preparing for a test, the hour plus was the optimal time for him to spend on his studies.   He knew that his mom disagreed.   If it were up to her, he'd spend three or four hours a night doing homework.   He also knew that, were it not for his mom's nagging, he would have been quite content to spend no more than just a few minutes a night studying.   The hour and a half was the result of major compromises on both sides.   Since he had been putting in the study time, he had seen his grades improve nearly every year until now he was among the top twenty percent of the students in his class.   He felt confident that as long as he could maintain that class rank and continue to become a better athlete, he would have a good chance to earn a scholarship.

CHAPTER 4

Preparing for a Dream

Each night when he had finished studying, Danny would put away his clothes, do the few chores he was required to do, and then head downstairs into the cellar, his private sanctuary. There he would spend close to an hour lifting weights (one night would be devoted to his legs, and the next night Danny would work on his upper body).

Coach French, the offensive line coach and a fanatic on weight lifting, had set up a program for him as well as a number of his friends. At Rockland, every player was required to lift weights in the off-season, but except for a fifteen-minute-a-day maintenance program, in-season lifting was optional. Danny had become more motivated to lift weights as he noticed his own strength and endurance improving. His coaches all encouraged him, and his friends were beginning to comment about his increase in both size and strength. It made Danny feel good when he heard from a teammate or another classmate pass on a compliment the coaches or a classmate. Danny would never have admitted it, but he was certain that several of the really cute girls in his class were becoming friendlier as his biceps started to bulge and his baby fat began to disappear.

During the past three years, Danny's grandfather, Gunther Evans (whose friends insisted on calling him "Red" despite the off-white color of what little hair still decorated his head) had gathered a large collection of weighted plates

16

barbells and constructed a makeshift gym in his grandson's cellar. There was a well-worn bench attached to a metal stand designed to hold the weighted bar that Danny used for the bench press. He was currently working with a hundred pounds, and could manage three sets of ten using that much weight. He maxed out at a hundred and eighty, though he was pretty sure he could get one-ninety (at least one time) if he had a spotter on hand to prevent a possible disaster. He figured he might go for it when his friend Matt Black came over to lift with him after church next Sunday.

The next morning at breakfast, Danny caught his mom humming softly to herself. When he asked her why she seemed so happy, she smiled and said, "Oh, do I seem happy? It must be because I'm having breakfast with my wonderful son, the light of my life." His mom often said things like that, so Danny didn't bother to question her further. Instead, he grabbed another hard roll and headed out the door. "Bye Mom," he said. "Have a good day."

"You too, dear," she said, as she waved him off.

Now Danny was certain something was different! His mom never said things like, "You too, dear." The two of them went through the same routine every day, every single day without exception. Danny would always say: "Bye Mom. Have a good day." This was his Mom's cue. She would always say, in a sort of mock argument: "No. *You* have a good day." Then Danny would answer back as if in final protest: "No, *you* have a good day." After this exchange, depending upon how silly she would decide to get, she would either repeat her command to have a good day, or simply give in by saying something to the effect: "Okay, wise guy, you win. I'll have a good day."

Her answer this morning would make him wonder frequently throughout the day what was happening in his mother's life to so preoccupy her. He was in fact wondering about his mother when the final school bell rang.

CHAPTER 5

Rumors of a Scout

At practice that afternoon, the last one the squad would run through before their season opener with Valley East, the locker room was buzzing. Everyone on the team knew that by the end of the practice, the coaches would have posted a list of who would be on the traveling squad to make the trip to Valley East on Saturday. Essentially, those boys whose names were posted on that list would comprise the varsity. Rockland dressed both the varsity and junior varsity squads for home games. That meant that usually there were no less than sixty boys in uniform. However, Coach Kirk never took more than thirty-six boys to the away games. Only the boys who were likely to play made the traveling squad. In all the years he had been the head coach at Rockland, excluding his very first year when only twenty-three boys had come out for the team, Coach Kirk had strictly adhered to this rule.

Except for Coach Kirk's first season when five freshmen actually stayed with the varsity all year, only two other boys had ever earned their varsity letters as freshmen. One was Bo James, and the other was a player from a time before Danny had even been born. His name was Steve Mitman. The rumor was that this week he had come back to Rockland to visit his old coach and his old school, specifically to scout Bo James, and possibly to offer him an athletic scholarship to the University of Michigan (Penn State's arch rival).

19

Because it was Friday, the day before the game, the team's uniform was shoulder-pads, shorts, helmet, and practice jersey. The workout began with the same calisthenics Coach Kirk planned to use in the pregame warm-up versus Valley East.

The team then did a modified set of agility drills (it was only a fraction of the number they normally did to warm up). When they finished, they broke up into groups. The offensive linemen: guards and tackles (but not the centers) went with Coach French to review their blocking assignments. Together they would practice pulling out of the line to lead the block on the power sweeps that went around end, or trap block on running plays that went inside the tackles. Then they met with the defensive linemen who had been practicing their own techniques with the defensive coordinator, Coach Johnson. The defense would then line up across from the offense, and they'd take turns practicing the moves and skills that each player would need to use during the game. It was a highly organized and very effective way to run a pregame practice.

Meanwhile, the centers would take turns acting as either long-snappers or short-snappers for the punters, and extra point and field goal kickers. While that was going on, the quarterbacks, wingbacks, tight ends, and wide receivers (split ends and flankerbacks), would run pass patterns against the defensive secondary (linebackers, defensive safeties and defensive halfbacks or cornerbacks).

Danny played tight end on offense, but Coach Wilson instructed him to begin the pregame workout with the linebackers. Both Fred Hogan, a second team outside linebacker, and Jason Jarrett, a sophomore who was a good prospect to be a backup for Bo James, had been injured in a scrimmage the week before. The trainer told Coach Kirk that Jarrett, who had a severely strained knee, might be back in two to three weeks, but Hogan, who had suffered a separated shoulder, would likely miss at least the first four to six weeks. This meant that Danny would be moved from the fourth to the third team on the defensive depth chart, and although he knew that it was far from a certainty (especially since he was only a fourteen-year-old freshman), there was a chance that he might make the traveling squad. Danny didn't like the idea of backing into anything. He preferred earning the chance to play, and he certainly wasn't happy to see a teammate injured. Even so, he couldn't help hoping that he might make the varsity squad as a freshman.

The practice shifted to the specialty teams. The kickoff team, the kickoff return team, the punt team, the punt return team, the extra point and field goal teams, and even the onsides kick team reviewed their personnel and what was expected of them. Danny was listed as second team on both the kickoff team and the punt team. He understood his assignments and his positioning on both teams.

When they had finished a run-through with every specialty team, the squad reviewed the defensive alignments, assignments, stunts and blitzes that they planned to use in their defensive package against Valley East. They finished by having the first three offensive teams run through every play in the offensive game plan against

Valley East's vaunted split-six defense. Coach Kirk and his staff were more than thorough, they were meticulous. It was only after they had covered every conceivable situation and reviewed every probable situation that might arise that they called the team together for a final word.

As was his custom, Coach Kirk spoke only briefly to the squad the night before a game. He saved his often-fiery speeches for the pregame get-together. He preferred that his team captains did most of the talking the night before the game.

Tonight the coach spoke briefly about the importance of getting off to a good start to the season. He reminded the team of the toughness of their opponent, and told them that he expected all of them to stay at home from ten o'clock the night before the game until they were ready to go to the stadium the next morning. The coaching staff then left the field, allowing the captains to speak to the squad without any of the coaches present.

First Hank "the Tank" Harmon addressed the team. He talked about how much he had looked forward to this, his senior season, and how he had been pointing to this season from the time he entered the first grade. He spoke of how all of them had worked so hard in the off-season getting ready for this. His message was plain and simple: They had sacrificed too much and come too far to lose. They needed to dig down deep and make certain they were ready to give whatever it took to reach their personal and collective goals. The team was still nodding in agreement when Bo James began to speak. He started softly, but his teammates hung on his every word. What he said had to do with teamwork. It had to do with picking each other up if one of them went down. It had to do with caring about each other the way you would care about your own family. He ended his talk by thrusting his hand towards the rest of his teammates and asking them a question they had all already answered with their eyes: "Are you guys with me?" The roar that followed assured him (as well as the coaches all the way across the street in the stadium) that indeed they were. The Rockland Warriors were as ready as they could possibly be. Bring on Valley East!

CHAPTER 6

The Surprise

Even as he jogged across the street with his teammates, Danny was becoming concerned about his chances of making the varsity. He had gone from being very confident of making the squad, to somewhat uncertain, and now finally to fearful that he would not make the varsity, at least not the traveling squad. He dreaded the possibility that all of his hopes were about to be sunk by what was missing from a sheet of paper—his name.

Time had flown. During the summer it seemed like the season might never come, but here it was—the Friday before the first varsity game of his freshman year. Apprehensively, Danny Cannon dragged himself across the practice field and then slowly shuffled down the long corridor to face the bulletin board on the wall across from the coaches' office.

Suddenly a voice from across the way snapped Danny from his mental fog: "What's wrong with you, Cannon?" It was Coach Wilson.

"Nothing, Coach," said Danny. "I'm just going to check the roster to see if I made the team."

"Made the team?" exclaimed Coach Wilson. "You better have made the team! I have you listed as my number two inside linebacker on the right side. Now you better just hustle on down to the equipment office and tell Mr.

Shockley (Bill Shockley was the team's equipment manager; he was the man in charge of handing out the game jerseys) that you need a jersey with a linebacker's number on it."

The grin that spread across Danny's face reminded Coach Wilson of a Maine sunrise he had seen one morning many years ago when he and his then-young bride had spent their honeymoon driving along the coastal highways of New England. It was a smile that spread from one side of Danny's face to the other and lit up the entire corridor. Danny sprinted down the hall like a thirsty horse to water. He relayed Coach Wilson's instructions to Bill Shockley and waited while the often-grumpy equipment manager began searching through the few game jerseys remaining in the bins.

"I have two left," he announced. "Number 83 and Number 88—both in large. I suppose you'll be wanting Number 88."

"Either one is okay," said Danny.

"Kid, don't you know nuthin'?" Bill Shockley asked.

"What do you mean?" Danny wanted to know.

"Don't you know that Number 88 was your grandad's number? Old Red wore Number 88. He made it famous, did your old grandpa. Don't you think old Red Evans would want his grandson to wear his old number? Course he would. I saved it for you, just in case you're half as good as old Red was."

"Nobody ever told me what my grandad's number was. I didn't think anybody even knew that he played football," replied Danny.

"Not know that old Red played! Heck, son, your grand-pappy was one of the greatest players ever to wear the Purple and White. Anybody who knows anything at all about Rockland football could have told you that. Not known about old Number 88? You can bet I do know about old Red!"

And so it was settled. Danny was handed his game gear, including his grandad's old jersey number, and the world seemed right.

Still walking on proverbial air, Danny showered, dried almost as an afterthought, and jogged most of the way home. No sooner was he in the house than his mom called him to the dinner table. Danny planned to wait until after supper and then surprise her by casually telling her the good news, using his best matter-of-fact voice. But he was so excited he could hardly eat his supper. He made a feeble effort to carry out his plan, but a few minutes into the meal he could wait no longer.

"Guess what?" Danny said, wearing his very best poker face.

"Give me a hint," his mother replied.

"Well, it has to do with the game tomorrow."

From the tone of his voice and way he had come through the front door that night, Nancy had long since surmised

26

her son's news. Still, she decided to play along with him. Putting on her best 'sympathetic mother' face she said, "Coach Kirk cut you from the squad. You're done with football forever."

Danny rolled his eyes. "Yeah, right, Mom."

"Do I get a second guess? she asked.

"Do you need one?"

"Well, let's see. If you didn't get cut from the team, and you aren't giving up football forever, my guess is that you made varsity and Coach is letting you dress for tomorrow's game."

"Oh Mom! Can't I ever surprise you?"

"Danny," she said, "you surprise me every day of my life!" and she hugged him greatly, messing up his hair as he pretended to struggle away.

CHAPTER 7

First-Game Butterflies

Danny decided to go to bed early in order to be ready for the game the next day, although he doubted he would sleep much that night. Danny was wrong. He slept like a rock.

Next morning, after a light breakfast, Nancy Cannon dropped her son off at the Rockland High School parking lot at 9:00. Danny had wanted to be there by 8:30, but his mother knew that 9:00 was more than enough time for Danny to get his gear together.

The team bus was scheduled to leave the Rockland High School parking lot at ten o'clock sharp. The bus ride was to take just a tad over an hour, but Coach Kirk always left his players plenty of time to get taped and dressed. Then there would be short meetings for the various position players with their own assistant coaches before the entire team got together with Coach Kirk for one of his famous pregame pep talks.

Danny didn't need to be taped. He had never worn any special pads the way many of the varsity players did, but this year Bo James himself mentioned the value of a forearm pad, so Danny had asked Bill Shockley if he could be issued one. Reluctantly, the surly equipment man found a battered old pad and issued it to Danny, saying that it was the only one he could find. When Bo James noticed it the night before, as Danny had pulled it over his forearm before the pregame practice, he questioned Danny about it and listened while Danny explained that it had been "the only forearm pad left."

Bo James simply smiled, nodded his head knowingly, asked Danny to give him the pad, and then vanished. A few minutes later, Bo James returned with a new forearm pad, as fine as the one he wore on his own arm.

Danny was appreciative and puzzled. Bo just smiled and replied that Bill Shockley had just remembered there was one new pad left. Danny wore the new pad with a great sense of pride. He felt a bit nervous, but excited and very ready to play.

What had seemed like an extremely long time to wait proved to be much shorter than Danny expected. Soon he was out on the field with his teammates, hustling through the pregame warm-ups. When he began to run through the passing lines with the offensive receivers, it was almost as if he had forgotten what he had learned in the many drills he had run through that summer. On his very first pass pattern, a short slant route across the middle, Danny dropped what should have been an easy catch. He realized he hadn't been concentrating on catching the ball the way he needed to in order to be a top receiver. His mind was on what the coach had told him as he was leaving the locker room. Coach Wilson had reached out and grabbed hold of one of his shoulder pads as he was going out the locker room door. "Be ready, Cannon," he had said. "I may need to use you at linebacker today."

Danny had been sort of in a daze since that moment. He was snapped out of his reverie by the voice of Coach Kirk. "Look the ball into your hands, Cannon," the coach called from behind the quarterback. "Concentrate on what you're doing, son."

Danny knew the coach was right. He shook himself mentally, and everything began to come into sharper focus.

Minutes later, Danny was working with Coach Wilson and the defensive unit. He was paired with Carl Shook. The two of them took turns stepping up aggressively and delivering a forearm shiver to each other's shoulder pads.

"Hey Danny, ease up, will ya?" Carl said. "Save those kind of hits for the game."

Danny hadn't realized the power behind the blow he had just delivered to Carl. The result was that he had staggered the reserve linebacker, nearly knocking him off his feet.

"Sorry." Danny mumbled. "I didn't realize that I hit you that hard."

"Yeah, sure," said Carl. "I guess you're just a born killer."

Danny smiled. The nervousness was beginning to fade, and he was feeling more aware of his surroundings. His senses were becoming sharper. He felt everything around him coming into clearer focus. It was as if a breeze had suddenly blown away a thick cloud of haze that had been covering the field. Danny Cannon felt ready to go. If only he would get the chance, he was certain he would do well today.

From that point until the opening kickoff, Danny grew more and more confident that he would do well. He didn't know why, but he just seemed to sense that today was to be his day.

Rockland lost the toss of the coin, and Valley East elected to receive the football. Rags McKenzie boomed the ball to the three-yard line. Before the Valley East kickoff return man could get underway, a Rockland tackler smashed him to the earth at his own eighteen-yard line. Three plays netted only four yards, and Valley was forced to kick on the fourth down. The punt was nearly blocked, and it spun crazily off the Valley punter's foot at the Valley East thirty-seven-yard line.

From there, the Big Dog carried twice for nine yards, and on third and one, Bo James blasted off tackle for a twenty-eight yard touchdown. The rout was on. By half-time Rockland led thirty-five to nothing. Early in the third quarter Bo James scored his fourth TD of the game, and Coach Kirk pulled his star fullback. The coach was already substituting freely on defense, and as the third quarter came to an end, with Rockland leading forty-two to six, Danny Cannon finally got his chance.

Coach Wilson sent the young freshman in for Mel Freeman at inside linebacker. On the first play Danny came up hard and brought the Valley fullback down after a gain of a yard. On second down, the desperate Valley quarterback started to scramble deep in his own territory. Hank Harmon stuck his big paw up just as the unfortunate Valley quarterback was in the process of throwing to his tight end on a short crossing pattern. The result was like the "tip drill" they had practiced so often during the summer. Danny saw the ball pop high into the air in front of him. He headed for it at the line of scrimmage, and caught it in full stride. He picked up a convoy of Rockland blockers almost immediately, and waltzed untouched into the Valley end zone thirty-three yards later. The stands on the Rockland side of the field, already jubilant, exploded in appreciative applause as if Danny's touchdown was the seal of victory.

Danny came off the field grinning. His teammates slapped him on the back and yelled congratulations. Coach Wilson mussed Danny's hair and winked at him, and Coach Kirk himself gave him an "Attaboy, Cannon" (high praise from the legendary coach).

Danny's first varsity football game had been a roaring success. He wondered why he had ever doubted himself. This varsity football was not nearly so tough as he thought it was going to be. The bus ride back was great. There was singing, joking, and general jubilation.

After all, Valley East had always been one of Rockland's toughest opponents. Could the Warriors really be that good? The answer wouldn't be long in coming. Central Penn was next on the schedule. Before they had the chance to completely digest their opening victory, the bus driver informed Coach Kirk that Central had just thumped

Marshfield 33-0. A frown darkened Coach's brow. Marshfield always played rock solid defense. They were not always a powerhouse like Rockland, but they rarely gave up more than a couple of touchdowns in a single game. No, Coach didn't like the sound of that score; he didn't like it at all.

Nancy met Danny in the school parking lot. Grandad Red was with her. They honked at Danny as he got off the bus. Danny had already showered, but he still had to hang his equipment up to dry before he could leave. He told his mom he'd be right back, and headed for the team's equipment room, equipment in hand.

Halfway to the team room Bill Shockley intercepted him. "Great game, kid," he called to Danny. "Where are you headin' with the gear?"

Danny smiled back at him. "I'm taking it to the team room to dry" he said.

"Give it to me," said the tall, thin manager. "I'll hang it up for you."

"Gee, thanks a lot," said Danny. "You sure you want to do that?"

"Sure kid," said Shockley. "Have a good time. And, tell your grandad I said 'hi.'"

Danny decided he liked being a celebrity; it had its perks. Apparently being treated like a star was one of them. Danny tried to imagine what it might be like to be Bo

James, but he found it impossible. *Man,* he thought to himself, *it sure would be great to be the hometown hero.*

CHAPTER 8

Postgame Celebration

Grandad Red was in a festive mood. He took Danny and his mom to Bellissimo's Pizza House and Restaurant. It was where the avid fans went after all the football games, or at least after all the victories. Many of Danny's teammates were already there. Some of the juniors and seniors had brought their dates, but most of them had come with their parents or large groups of friends. All having a great time.

Tony and Frank Giordano, the two brothers who owned the place, always bought the first pitcher of soda for the team players. Occasionally they'd also send a complimentary pizza or a special dessert to players who had played exceptionally well. It was rumored that Bo James never paid a cent when he came to the pizza house, but there were so many stories and rumors about Bo James, few people knew which were true.

When the waitress finally took their order, she smiled at Danny. "Nice game, kid," she said. "Frank and Tony told me you were the next Bo James."

Red ordered a large pizza with pepperoni and sausage and Danny's mom asked to have mushrooms and green peppers added. Danny opted for a giant cheese steak with onions, peppers and all the trimmings. The waitress brought them a pitcher of Coke, and several of Danny's teammates waved hello. When dinner came, Tony Giordano himself came to their table. A former offensive tackle who had done his playing more than twenty years earlier, Tony loved to be associated with Rockland sports, especially the football program.

"Eat hearty, kid," he said. "You need to keep getting bigger if you're gonna play for State. You looked good in there today—real good. The sandwich and soda is on the house; you deserve it." Then he turned to Danny's grandfather, smiled and said, "The kid's a chip off the old block, Red. He's a winner just like his grandad. Enjoy your meal."

Not wanting to leave out Danny's mom, he turned to her, still smiling. "Nice to see you, Mrs. Cannon. You got a real athlete there. Stop by more often." Then he walked away.

Red Evans just shook his head. "He's a real fair weather fan," said Danny's grandfather.

"What do you mean by that?" Danny wanted to know. "He seemed nice enough."

"Oh, he's nice enough, leastwise long as you're winning," said Red Cannon. "Trouble is, in sports, sometimes you lose."

Danny was going to ask his grandad to explain how Tony would change when a big, athletic-looking man wearing a short sleeved white shirt and a navy blue tie approached their table. Danny noted the stranger's muscular physique. The man was smiling in their direction, but Danny noticed

36

that he appeared to be looking more at Nancy Cannon than at his grandfather or at him.

"Hello Nancy. Hello Red, I saw the game. Looks like one day I might just be scouting this young man. Nice game, son."

Danny looked from the stranger to his mom, then across the table at his grandfather. All three were smiling broadly and appeared to know one another.

Nancy spoke up. "Hello, Steve. I don't think you've met my son, Danny. Danny, I want you to meet an old friend of mine from high school, Steve Mitman."

Steve stuck out his hand in Danny's direction. Danny thrust his hand forward politely, and noticed that his hand sort of disappeared in the man's big hand.

"Good to meet you Danny. You played a fine game today. Rockland looks like they'll be plenty tough to beat this year. What did you think about the game, Red?"

Danny's grandfather continued to smile. "Looks like it'll take a good team to beat them all right. But there's always lots of good teams up here in the mountains."

"That's for sure," said Steve. "Still, not every team has Bo James as its running back."

"I guess that's why you're here, isn't it?" asked Red.

"Well, it's certainly one of my reasons."

"Oh, are there other reasons?" asked Red.

"There are," said Steve, "but that's about all I can tell you, at least for right now." Nancy invited Steve to sit with them. He politely declined, explaining that he had already eaten and was on his way to a pressing business engagement. He did, however, ask Danny's mother for a rain check, and he left with an invitation from Nancy to come for dinner the next time he came to town. Steve assured Nancy that he would be happy to accept her offer.

Danny hadn't seen his mother so animated for a long time. It was good to see her happy. He wondered if Steve, this old friend of hers, might be someone special. He was in the midst of speculating about his mother's feelings when the food arrived. His grandfather handed him a slice of pizza as well as the steak sandwich he had ordered. Playing varsity football gave a fella a real appetite. For awhile Danny forgot about everything except how good the food tasted. It was a night to enjoy the victory of that day.

CHAPTER 9

A Visit from the Snake and the Big Bear

On Monday Coach Kirk acted more like the Warriors lost than won. At the film session at the end of practice, he was quick to point out the many mistakes the team made on Saturday. Danny had expected to suit up for the junior varsity game that Rockland was to play at 7:00 P.M. Instead, he was told by Coach Wilson that, for the time being he would be staying with the varsity. That meant that he would not be permitted to play in the J.V. games, at least not for the present. With injuries still sidelining two of the varsity's key upperclassmen at the linebacker position, Danny was needed to provide depth. His welfare couldn't be risked in a junior varsity game.

Although Danny would have liked to play in the J.V. games, where he would have been starting at both linebacker and offensive end, he felt honored that the varsity coaching staff considered him too valuable to be risking injury in a junior varsity game. Danny wondered if he would play in the next varsity game. It wouldn't be long before he would be given more of an opportunity than even he had hoped for.

Saturday night was to be Rockland's home opener against a Central Penn team that many sportswriters had begun tabbing as a legitimate contender for the Pennsylvania

Mountain Conference championship. The Raiders had a big offensive line that had manhandled the tough Marshfield defense the week before. They ran a wing-T that featured a fine passer in Jake "the Snake" Ferrintino and a wingback with blazing speed (Nick "the Quick" Karras was timed at 4.4 seconds in the 40-yard dash). In addition, they had an outstanding defense. The Central Penn coach had praised his team as being "mobile, agile, and hostile" after they shut out Marshfield the preceding week. They were led by one of the best defensive ends in the Keystone State— Ted Jacobs.

"The Big Bear" as Jacobs had been dubbed by the press, recorded twelve unassisted tackles and four quarterback sacks in week one, despite being double-teamed on nearly every play by Marshfield. Coach Kirk warned his squad that Central Penn was "for real" and that if the Warriors were to enter the game the least bit overconfident, it would be a fatal mistake. At their pregame practice both Bo James and Hank Harmon had re-emphasized Coach Kirk's warnings. They told the team in no uncertain terms that Central Penn was as good as the newspapers were reporting them to be.

Danny listened to every word both his coach and the team captains said. He was sure that Rockland would be ready to take on the Raiders. He couldn't have been more wrong.

Things started out nightmarish for the Warriors. Big Dog Perez bobbled the opening kickoff and then tried to make up for it by running opposite the wall his teammates formed on the left side of the field. When he was hit

40

simultaneously by two big Central Penn defenders, the ball popped loose, and though Perez had struggled to recover his fumble, the Raiders came up with it inside the Rockland ten-yard line. It seemed like the Warriors might survive when Bo James and Hank Harmon stopped the Raiders for no gain on two successive plays. But then, on third and goal from the ten, despite being under a heavy pass rush, Jake "the Snake" wriggled free deep in his own backfield and sped for the far corner of the end zone. Bo James tore halfway across the field and dove to keep him out of pay dirt, but the snake stretched the ball across the pylons before being driven out of bounds. The Central Penn kicker sent the extra point straight through the uprights, and before the capacity crowd had even settled into their seats, the Warriors trailed 7-0.

The Purple and White marched down the field on what seemed to be a determined drive of their own. Bo James was carrying on nearly every play. It was evident that the Central Penn coaching staff had done their scouting well. They assigned their best linebacker to act as a "monster" on Bo. He shadowed him on every play, and together with a hard-hitting defensive line, he was able to keep the Warrior star from breaking off any huge gains. Still, the determined Rockland running back was ripping off gains of five and six yards at a clip, and it looked like that might be good enough to counter the Raiders' early touchdown. On fourth and goal at the Central Penn six, Bo took a pitchout and started around left end. The Raiders reacted as if they had a spy in the Warriors' huddle. It seemed as if every Central Penn defensive lineman had slid a gap to the right. They were there in a solid wall to meet Bo. The powerful back smashed into the pile, but when it did not give an inch, he spun back in the opposite direction.

Heading back to his own right, he encountered Ted "Big Bear" Jacobs at the three-yard line. Bo lowered his shoulder and smashed into the mammoth defender, driving him back a step or two. At the one, the hard-charging Bo stretched for the goal line. Just as the official threw his hands in the air, signaling touchdown, the Raiders' fast-pursuing monster back crashed into Bo The resulting crunch could be heard throughout the stadium. The three players seemed welded into a human scrap heap. When they were finally untangled, all three boys remained on the ground. Bo was the first to stir. He tried valiantly to stand, but could not. The officials signaled time out and waved the trainers and team doctor onto the field.

The Warriors had tied the score, but Bo James had to be helped off of the field by two of his teammates. Likewise, "Big Bear" Jacobs needed to be helped off. The Raider monster back finally came 'round, but he too was taken out of the game. None of the three would return that night. The entire season for Bo James appeared to be in doubt. A terrible hush fell over the crowd.

With their star player missing, the Warriors played lackluster football the rest of the way. Fortunately for them, the equally disheartened Raiders played even more sluggishly. With just over two minutes to go in the game, Skeeter Simms, a fleet Rockland wingback, caught a pass out in the flat, and sped all the way to the Central Penn nine-yard line.

Three plays later, facing a fourth and goal at the eight, Coach Kirk opted to try a field goal. Rags McKenzie kicked it through and then, led by an emotional Ross Tanner, the defense stopped a frantic comeback bid by Jake "the Snake" and his Raiders. The final score read Rockland 10, Visitors 7. Bo James was out indefinitely. It was a costly victory for the Warriors.

CHAPTER 10

A Team Sport

Danny got into the game only on the kickoffs, and with Bo James apparently seriously injured, the victory seemed a joyless one. The Rockland team and their fans were discouraged. What had seemed like a championship season was now in jeopardy.

On Monday, Coach Kirk addressed the team in the locker room before practice. Bo James had suffered a torn cartilage in his left knee, and had badly strained the ligament as well. He would undergo arthroscopic surgery that afternoon. Even if it was successful, they could expect him to be out a minimum of four weeks, and if and when he returned, it would take a while for him to get back to full strength. That meant that it was likely Bo James would miss most, if not all, of the season.

Anticipating the team's reaction, Coach Kirk immediately explained what needed to be done. First, he made every player aware of how critical it was to practice even harder. No single player was going to be able to replace Bo James. Instead, the coach would expect each starter to play between five and ten percent better than he had when Bo James was in the lineup. Likewise, each substitute would need to improve more rapidly, and every single one of them would be expected to pick up a bit of the slack that Bo's absence would cause.

44

Danny noticed that as Coach Kirk spoke, each player, beginning with the starters and the seniors, and soon spreading to the juniors and the underclassmen, had begun nodding his head in agreement with the plan. By the time Coach had finished, a new sense of team spirit pervaded the locker room. The pessimism and the general discouragement had been driven out by a newfound hope, and that hope appeared to have been bolstered by grim determination and the resurgence of Rockland pride.

By Friday, the Coach meshed all of the pieces. The starting offensive lineup had the following major changes: Bo James would be replaced at right halfback by Enrico Perez; the Big Dog's left halfback position would be taken over by Skeeter Simms; and finally, Tim Kern would move up to the starting wingback position to replace Skeeter Simms.

On defense, Hank Harmon would call the defensive signals from his tackle position. Chuck Crandall would move from weak side to strong side linebacker replacing Bo James, and Danny Cannon, previously Crandall's backup, would move into the starting lineup at weak side linebacker. Danny was excited. He wasn't at all afraid for his own safety, but he was scared to death that he might let his teammates down. That night Danny thought about Coal Mountain, the team he would be expected to stop the next day. He thought about Bo James, and what it must have been like for him to start on the varsity as a freshman. He thought about his grandfather; he knew that Red Evans was filled with pride that his grandson had made the starting

45

team his freshman year. He thought about how much he needed to earn a scholarship, so his mother wouldn't need to worry about paying his college tuition. He thought about playing in front of the huge crowd that would fill the Miners' stadium the next day. Danny whispered a quick prayer that he wouldn't embarrass himself and his family, that he wouldn't disappoint anyone who was counting on him. Danny didn't sleep well that night. He barely slept at all.

○   ○   ○

The next morning Coach Wilson made it a point to sit Danny next to Chuck on the bus ride up to Coal Mountain. Danny was told to ask questions concerning any of the defenses that Rockland planned to run against the Miners. Many teams ran simple defenses with little movement between the line and linebackers, but Rockland ran a sophisticated system that involved stunts, slants, loops and blitzes. The line needed to learn three or four basic defensive techniques and a half a dozen moves calling for a specific defensive maneuver. However, the linebackers worked both in conjunction with the line and in tandem with the defensive secondary as well as with each other. When Bo James played the strong side linebacker, there were as many as a dozen different moves and twice that many defensive "looks" that he might call in his defensive game plan. Coach Wilson had simplified that game plan for Hank Harmon, and he had made certain that Danny and Chuck Crandall understood exactly what each was required to do in any given defensive set and maneuver. Because of Danny's lack of experience, most of the time he would be the more aggressive of the two linebackers. This meant that on the stunts, blitzes, loops and fires, he would be crashing into the opponents' backfield. Chuck Crandall would usually be expected to do the more difficult job of "reading" backfield flow and offensive line movement and then using his understanding of what these moves signaled to make his own adjustments. To the average fan, it would appear that Danny was the tougher and more aggressive linebacker. In reality, Danny was made to look like a hero, even if he made a mistake. Chuck needed to back off and react to the flow, being sure to read correctly the opposing team's every signal.

It was a great way for the coaches to cover for Danny's lack of experience while making full use of his enthusiasm, his aggressiveness, and his willingness to throw his body recklessly into the fray. Against the hard-nosed Coal Mountain running game, the defensive scheme worked like a charm.

CHAPTER 11

Cannon Shot

Early in the game, Rockland marched nearly eighty yards on just nine plays. The Big Dog scored the go-ahead touchdown on a special play designed to outflank the tough Coal Mountain defenders. On third and six from midfield, Coach Kirk called for the offensive line to shift to an unbalanced right formation. The play was called 100 Double Strong, Jet Right. Designed especially to take advantage of the speed of the Big Dog, the play actually enabled the Warriors to outflank their opponent by flopping the backside end to the strong side of the formation. The strong side guard would pull and act as a personal escort for the right halfback. When the strong safety came up hard to attempt to stop the pitch, Sharky Sellman greeted him with a crunching shoulder block that knocked him off his feet. That was all that the Big Dog needed. He high-stepped his way forty-eight yards down the sidelines and into the end zone. Rags McKenzie split the uprights to make it 7 to 0, and that is how it stayed until late in the second quarter.

With just three and a half minutes remaining till halftime, Coal Mountain caused the Warriors to punt from their own twenty-eight yard line. Then the Miners began a relentless drive of their own. Taking over at their thirty-three-yard line, they used Shawn Steigerwalt, a battering ram of a fullback, mixed with the outside threat of Sly Nelson, to

48

drive to the Rockland twelve. There on third and seven, the Coal Mountain coach decided to run his star fullback on a draw play up the middle. With most of the Rockland team thinking pass, it might have worked, but Danny had been assigned to fire the gap between the center and the left guard while the defensive nose tackle, Mike Bowers, slanted into the gap just to his left. The center and the right guard lunged to pick up the slanting Bowers. The left guard, seeing Chuck Crandall drop into his pass coverage lane, sealed him off to create a running lane for his big fullback. Unfortunately for Coal Mountain, they hadn't counted upon the low-flying Danny Cannon to make his presence felt. Unblocked and in full stride, the freshman sparkplug hit the outstretched arm of the Coal Mountain quarterback just as he attempted to slip the ball into the waiting arms of his quick-pivoting fullback. The timing of Danny's unimpeded blitz couldn't have been better for Rockland, or more disastrous for Coal Mountain. The football squirted into the air and the impact of Danny's soon-to-be-labeled "Cannon Shot" caused the fullback and quarterback to crash into each other. Hank Harmon scooped up the pigskin and rumbled more than raced eighty plus yards for a touchdown. Neither team could mount anything resembling a sustained drive after that, and as a result the final score read Rockland 14, Coal Mountain 0.

Danny knew he should be happy that he contributed to his team's victory, but instead he felt as if he had somehow betrayed his teammates by geting so much attention from the fans. He was uneasy on the team bus, and still dejected when he arrived home late that afternoon.

Nancy was beaming when Danny walked through the door. His grandfather had invited them to share dinner with him at Bellissimo's, and of course Danny's mom was sure he would be pleased. Instead, Danny was confused and a bit disappointed. He had expected there to be more, somehow. He should have been proud and happy, but he felt empty and strangely guilty.

Danny would have preferred to spend the night at home with just his mother, but he knew how disappointed both she and Red would feel if they knew how he felt, so he agreed to go to dinner with them. He would later wish he had stayed at home.

○   ○   ○

Bellisimo's was jumping. It seemed that most of the team had decided to celebrate victory there. Both Frank and Tony Giordano visited Danny's table, congratulating him and once again sending over complimentary pitchers of soda and large quantities of pizza together with Danny's cheese steak. They refused to hear of Red paying for anything. Danny was fast replacing the injured Bo James as the newest Rockland celebrity-hero. Danny had grown up believing in the concept of teamwork. He was completely unselfish, to the point that it bothered him to be given so much credit for doing what he believed was no more than his assigned responsibility on the football field. He was confused and more than a bit embarrassed by all the attention and accolades the press had been giving him. He just wanted to play football and do his part to help his team win games.

Sunday the headline across the sports page of *The Rockland Express* read: "Cannon Shot Lifts Warriors Past Miners." And the feature story said: "The Rockland Warriors replaced the explosive missile-like runs of star running back Bo James with new and effective artillery fire. Hank 'the Tank' Harmon teamed with freshman sensation Danny 'Big Boom' Cannon to lead the wounded, but none-the less dangerous Rockland Warriors to a hard-fought 14-0 victory over the Coal Mountain Miners Saturday at Miner's Memorial Stadium. In what proved to be the game's pivotal play, freshman Danny Cannon crashed into the Miner backfield and wreaked havoc with the attempted handoff. Warrior's co-captain Hank Harmon scooped up the fumble and rumbled coast to coast with the pigskin to extend the Warrior lead to 13-0. Reliable Rags McKenzie split the uprights with his tenth consecutive extra point, and that was all the scoring needed as a rock-ribbed Warrior defensive unit made the two touchdowns stand up for the Warriors third straight victory without a defeat."

The newspaper was lavish in its praise of both Hank and Danny, but the modest ninth grader felt uncomfortable because the newspaper failed to mention the outstanding linebacker play of Chuck Crandall. Also lost in the shuffle was the touchdown run of "Big Dog" and the unselfish play of Rockland's hard-hitting defensive line. Danny felt guilty about having received the lion's share of the ink.

At school on Monday, Danny noticed that his peers had begun to treat him differently. He was a hero in the eyes of his freshmen classmates. Guys who a few weeks earlier hadn't so much as known his name, now spoke to him in the hallway as if they were longtime friends. Girls who hadn't given him a second look now smiled at him, and some flirted openly, causing him to blush and stammer a little when they spoke to him.

Even his teachers appeared to have a new respect for him. Ms. Larrimer mentioned to the biology class that they had a "celebrity in their midst" and had gone on to praise Danny's performance on the football field. Even the usually grouchy Ms. Juniper smiled at him when she signed his pass, and wished him luck in the upcoming game against Marshfield.

Modesty prevented Danny from enjoying his newfound fame. Still, he began to feel that perhaps he had under-valued himself. After all, if everyone else believed he was a star, who was he to disagree? Danny was almost convinced that he might be the next Bo James when Coach Kirk called the Warriors together that Monday after practice to review the game films from the previous Saturday.

Until then, Danny had never had so much as a word of criticism directed his way from any of the coaches. Perhaps that was because Coach Kirk had realized Danny's ego was much too fragile to be able to withstand the criticism that most upperclassmen had come to accept as a part of the game.

Now, however, Danny would find out that together with the many rewards and accolades that came with varsity sports, there also came critical comments that enabled veteran varsity athletes to become aware of their errors and to correct them. Thus it seemed that, in the eyes of Coach Kirk, Danny's performance the past Saturday had been riddled with mistakes, the type of mistakes that had caused the freshman to hesitate when decisive action was called for. His errors had most often been errors of omission. At times it was Danny's hesitation that had his teammates covering up for his slow reactions to developing plays, while at other times he had simply assumed the wrong responsibility on a defensive maneuver. It wasn't so much that Danny had done the wrong thing, but rather he had created situations that could have resulted in problems for the Warriors. Coach Kirk pointed out, for instance, that on one play where Danny had sacked the Coal Mountain quarterback for a six-yard loss, his primary responsibility had been to cover the tight end who was running a delaying pattern across the middle of the field. Fortunately, the Warriors' other inside linebacker had covered the receiver long enough for Danny to make the tackle. Even so, it was the tight end who was Danny's responsibility on the play, and the Warriors had been lucky that the results of that play turned out as they did; otherwise the momentum of the game could have changed.

By the time the coach had reviewed the game film with the squad, Danny no longer had a swollen head. In fact, he was worried about still having a starting position on the varsity. When Coach sent word via Bill Shockley that he was to stop by Coach Kirk's office before leaving for home that night, Danny was worried.

CHAPTER 12

For the Good of the Team

Danny walked the long, cold corridor that led from the players' locker room to Coach Kirk's office with a feeling of trepidation mixed with resignation. He was afraid that the coach was going to tell him that he would no longer be playing with the varsity, but he had resigned himself to accepting his impending demotion as positively as he knew how. Timidly Danny knocked on the door to the Coach's office.

"Come in," said Coach Kirk. "I need to talk with you."

The first part of the conversation confirmed Danny's worst fears. Fred Hogan had made a speedy recovery from his injuries, and Coach Kirk had decided to start him at linebacker. The coach explained that Hogan was older and more experienced, and would have been starting ahead of Danny had he not been injured. Danny's spirits sagged. He realized what the coach was saying was fair, and it made sense. Still he wanted to plead his case, but he realized that it would be selfish to do so; instead he just nodded his head as Coach Kirk continued.

"There's a J.V. game tonight. I'd like you to play in it. I want to see what you can do at offensive end. We don't have the scoring punch we need on the varsity. We need a receiver we can count on. I think that if you're allowed to concentrate more on offense and less on defense, you could be that receiver. I want to see how you do in the J.V. game first. You'll still be with the varsity on Saturday. You'll back up Fred Hogan at linebacker, but you'll also be alternating with Mark Sheridan at split end." Danny was speechless. Suddenly there was a lot to do. He needed to call his mom to tell her that he would not be home for dinner because he was going to be playing in the J.V. game. He wanted to tell his grandfather, so his grandfather would be sure to come to the game. He needed to get a game uniform from Bill Shockley. He needed to get his gear together. He needed to get his left ankle taped. Tonight would be a night of many firsts.

His heart was pounding. He realized that what he needed to do most of all was relax and review his pass patterns. It had been weeks since he had studied them the way he should have. He had been too absorbed in learning his defensive calls, sets, and responsibilities to concentrate on the many pass patterns.

Danny called his mom at the school where she worked, explained that he would be playing in the J.V. game that evening, and would not be home until it was over, and he asked her to let his grandfather know his situation so that Red would be able to attend the game if he chose to do so. Then he proceeded to the locker room, playbook in hand.

An hour later, Danny sat on the trainer's table, pads in place, jersey pulled snugly down over his shoulder pads, and playbook open in front of him. He studied the pass patterns intently.

Coach Hohenstein was the junior varsity head coach, and Coach Tevarni assisted him. Danny knew them both only by sight at the practice sessions with the varsity. He hadn't had much contact with them, because he had been working with the varsity all season. It was Coach Hohenstein who came to Danny now.

"Hi, Danny," he began. "I'm Coach Hohenstein. We're glad to have you with us. Coach Kirk explained that he wants me to start you on offense to see what you can do. We probably won't use you at all on defense tonight unless we absolutely need to because of injuries. We already know you can play there.

"We want to throw the ball quite a bit tonight. Coal Mountain's J.V.'s haven't lost a game yet, but neither have we, so we're expecting a tough game. We'll keep the pass patterns pretty basic, but when we want to throw the ball, we'll be looking at you as a primary receiver on most plays. If any play is called that you're not clear on, ask Bobby Williams, our QB. He'll let you know your route."

By the time Coach Hohenstein had called the J.V.'s together for the pregame prayer and a few final words, Danny felt comfortable and confident. He was ready and eager to get started.

Coal Mountain won the coin toss and elected to receive. Six plays later, their wingback stood in the end zone looking for an official to toss the ball to. He had just zipped fifty-seven yards on a tricky reverse, and had practically gone untouched those last fifty.

The kicker booted the extra point through as if he had kicked PAT's his entire life, and so with only three minutes gone, the score read Visitors 7, Rockland 0.

Rockland's deep back mishandled the kickoff, and when the dust cleared, a Coal Mountain defender lay clutching the pigskin at the Rockland nineteen. On first down, the quarterback faked a dive to his fullback, then bellied down the line of scrimmage looking directly at the Rockland defensive end. When the end drove for the QB, the Coal Mountain field general tossed a soft pitch to the trailing halfback, who streaked the remaining distance into the end zone. The kick was once again perfect, and it looked pretty dim for the Rockland underclassmen.

On the ensuing kickoff, Rockland's deep man managed to get the ball back across his own twenty-five.

A fullback dive followed by a tailback slant off left tackle netted only three yards. On third and seven Coach Hohenstein sent a play in from the sidelines.

In the huddle Bobby Williams looked directly at Danny and then called the play: 100 tight, X-split, Z-out, flag and drag. This meant that there was to be a three-man pattern. On the right (the 100 side) the wingback would run a ten yard square out route and the tight end would drive down the field about twelve yards and then break sharply for the flag in the right corner of the end zone. Danny would be split eight yards to the left (the left end was designated as the X-receiver) and the right end the Y-receiver. The wingback (or flanker) was the

Z-receiver. To simplify the call, unless the tight end was to be split, in some unusual formation, the quarterback didn't need to refer to him by using the letter Y.

Danny was to watch the two Coal Mountain linebackers. If possible, he would run his route about 4-6 yards behind them, but if they read pass and dropped deep quickly, he would simply run an "underneath" route, one in which he would "drag" across the middle, trying to stay in the vacated area as much as possible.

The quarterback had his priorities numbered for him on each play. In this case, he would try to get the ball first to the wingback squaring out toward the sidelines. If he was covered, the QB's next choice would be to look a bit deeper in the same area at the tight end running a "flag pattern." If neither receiver was open, the quarterback was to look for the split end "delaying" and then "dragging" across the middle. If no one was open, the quarterback was told to tuck the football and run.

As luck would have it, Danny found himself wide open and running alone behind the two linebackers. Both the tight end and wingback were covered. Bobby just needed to throw him the ball, and he would have the yardage needed for the first down. The Warrior quarterback saw him, cocked his arm, and was ready to let the ball fly when a poorly blocked Coal Mountain defender blindsided the unsuspecting Rockland passer. The ball was jolted out of his arm and rolled toward the Warrior goal line. A Coal Mountain defensive end scooped it up and ran it into the end zone for the third Miner TD of the first quarter. The young Warriors were in a state of shock.

CHAPTER 13

The Born Leader

Danny Cannon looked around him. He had never been in this situation before. There was a mixture of fear and confusion in the eyes of his young teammates. For some reason, they seemed to be looking to him for leadership. Danny grinned. "I guess we can't do much worse than what we've done so far. Are you guys ready to start over?"

A resounding "Yeah," issued back at him. The team was with him. Now it was time to rebuild their confidence.

Danny wasn't in on the kickoff return team, but he spoke to "Mouse" Miller, the deep man. "You can do it, big guy," he said. "Relax. Follow your blockers." The little scat-back smiled and nodded his head. The kick came into his waiting arms at the five-yard line. Mouse followed the three-man wedge to about the twenty and then broke sharply to his left. For a minute, it looked as if he might break it all the way, but the kicker forced him out of bounds around midfield.

Bobby Williams went immediately to the air. A fullback screen picked up nine yards. Williams then fooled everybody by calling for a deep pass on second and one. "Slot-I Right, Fake Wham, Split End Streak" was his call. The sophomore signal caller faked a handoff to the tailback into the middle of the line, hid the ball on his right hip, and dropped deep and to his right. The right end ran a

60

right flag route, while the slotback cleared the deep safety by running a far post right past his nose. Danny knew that he would be covered man-to-man by the Coal Mountain weak side safety. To elude him, he needed either to outrun him or to find a way to rub him off as the slotback crossed the middle of the field. He had watched the defender closely and was pretty sure he wouldn't be able to outrun him, at least not by much. Instead, he decided to try to lose him by timing his cut to coincide with that of his slotback. When the ball was snapped, he drove hard off the line of scrimmage for about five yards. He then whipped his head and shoulders to the left as if he were going to head for the left flag. Instead, he pivoted on his right foot and broke sharply for his right. The maneuver provided him with a two- or three-yard advantage over the defender who found himself backpedaling. Danny took full advantage of the defender's mistake and opened up another three yards between himself and the safety. Danny never stopped watching the slot-back as he ran his crossing pattern. He knew that against a man-to-man coverage, his cuts would need to be particularly sharp and precise. They were.

As the far side safety stayed stride for stride with the fast-moving slotback, Danny cut hard between them and streaked for the near post in the end zone. His pursuer crashed headlong into the middle safety, and the two of them went down in a heap. Danny raised his left hand to help Bobby see that he was now wide open. Williams, who had been looking for him from the snap, lofted the ball in the direction of the goal line. Sometimes the easiest catches turn out to be the hardest, but not this time. Danny pulled the ball in at about the ten-yard line. He went into the end zone untouched. Rockland was on the scoreboard.

The try for extra point was blocked, but the Warriors were now fired up. By the end of the first half Rockland had scored twice more, once on a quarterback sneak from just a yard away, and once on a sixty-two-yard pass to Danny, who simply outran the entire Coal Mountain secondary for the score. Coal Mountain managed a touchdown and again made the PAT, so the score at halftime was Coal Mountain 28, Rockland 19.

In the second half, Rockland's defense stiffened, allowing only one more touchdown. Danny led the Warrior offense, which scored another 20 points, two on pass plays of more than fifty yards from Williams to Cannon. The final score stood at Rockland 39 and Coal Mountain 35. It was rare to have that much scoring in a JV game, and it left the fans buzzing about their young football hero—Danny Cannon.

At practice the next day, Coach Kirk made it a point to congratulate Danny on his contribution to the JV victory. More than a few of his JV teammates stopped by Danny's hall locker before homeroom to slap him on the back or comment about his performance the night before.

Tuesday, on the practice field, the Big Dog saw Danny and shook his head smiling. "Umm, umm, umm, my brother. If you ain't a touchdown makin' fool. I hear you the next Bo James. They say you the second comin'. I say you better watch out that the Cannon Man don't be no cannon fodder when he go against the big boys this week, if you get my meanin,' 'Bo Junior'."

Danny was always a bit embarrassed when an upper classman addressed him directly. He wasn't quite sure of what to make of the Big Dog, nor did he know whether comments were meant as a compliment or an insult. He guessed they were intended to keep him from getting a swollen head. They sounded like a warning, but if they were, the Big Dog didn't need to worry about Danny. He knew by now that to be the star of the J.V. game was one thing, but to make a contribution to a varsity victory was something entirely different. He wasn't about to let all the praise of his J.V. teammates, (or the Rockland fans and press for that matter) cause him to believe he was any better than he really was. On the other hand, Danny's inner confidence was growing stronger with every practice. He had reached the point where he felt that he could perform well enough on the varsity level to contribute to a Rockland victory. The coach knew what he was doing when he had told Danny to suit up and play in the J.V. game. Danny was now certain he knew his assignments, and he was anxious to prove he could play offense on the varsity level. Moreover, he was beginning to like playing offense even more than he had liked playing defense. He no longer feared making mistakes in front of the fans; he now hoped that the coach would call his number in a varsity game. He wanted the ball to be thrown to him. He was certain he wouldn't let his team, his coach, his family, or his friends

down. Danny knew he had better be ready; Marshfield
loomed on the horizon.

CHAPTER 14

The "C" Word

That week in school, the talk was about the Rockland Warriors and their chances for a championship. When Bo James had been injured, the hopes for a championship season seemed to have crumbled. But now, the pessimism of the Rockland fans gradually diminished. There were some who actually began to whisper that "C" word as Coach Kirk liked to call it. Coach Kirk refused even to mention the word "championship" when the press interviewed him. He was from the old school. He didn't just pay lip service to the old cliché of playing one game at a time. He refused to let his players even mention such an idea in his presence, though he was certainly well aware of what was on the minds of every Rockland player and fan. Not only was Coach Kirk strict, he was tough.

Secretly referred to by his players as "The Strap," because many years ago his own coach told reporters that John Kirk was "tougher than a leather strap," Coach Kirk had been around football his entire life. Now, at age fifty-two, he had become a living legend in Rockland. He had been the head coach of what he nearly single-handedly turned into the football Mecca of Eastern Pennsylvania for almost thirty years. He was now coaching many of the sons of his former players, and every one of them was thoroughly prepared for what to expect from "The Strap." The result was that Rockland had become synonymous with championship football, and expectations were always high. The pressure to win was great, but Coach Kirk had always felt that pressure. Long before community expectations had created it, the pressure had come from within. John Kirk never allowed what the fans or the news media said to cause him stress; the pressure from inside of him is what drove him. The will to win is what made him great. As he had often explained to his players: "It is not just wanting to win that makes a champion, because everyone who competes wants to win. The will to win is much more than just wanting to win. It is the will to make the necessary sacrifices that winning takes. The 'will to win' is the will to work hard to prepare to win. It is the will to dedicate yourself to a cause, and to sacrifice your own personal glory for the good of the team. That is what winning is all about. More importantly, that is what life is all about. That willingness to sacrifice in order to achieve a goal is what makes a champion. It is what makes a man."

Coach Kirk's players believed in him. They were loyal to him. Opposing coaches knew that if they were to beat Rockland, they would need to first break Rockland's spirit, and then either physically overwhelm them or outsmart them. With Coach Kirk leading the Warriors, it was next to impossible to outsmart them. With the Rockland players continually preparing themselves to win, other teams seldom had the talent to physically overpower them. The result was that year after year, Rockland found itself contending for the championship. The Rockland fans, like the Rockland players, expected no less.

Marshfield was not supposed to present any special problems for Rockland. Despite the warnings from Coach Kirk that Marshfield would be tough, the players read the newspapers. It was the newspapers who now touted Rockland as a "championship caliber football team" despite the injury to star running back Bo James. It was the newspapers who had predicted that Rockland "would have little trouble dispatching a weak Marshfield team." If they were overconfident going into the Marshfield contest, who could blame them? Marshfield had lost its opener 33-0 to Central Penn, a team Rockland had beaten 10-7. It had lost its next game 14-7 to Whitehall, and in its last outing had lost again (7-6 to Juniper Falls). What the newspapers saw was a team that had lost three games without winning one. What the Rockland players saw was a team that had been walloped 33-0 by Central Penn, a team they had already defeated. What Coach Kirk saw was an opponent who had been forced to start many young and inexperienced players. What the veteran coach saw was an opponent who was improving with every game. What Coach Kirk feared was an opponent his squad might take for granted. He knew that all of the ingredients for an upset were present. He also knew that unless he could convince his football team that Marshfield was a dangerous opponent, his squad was going to be in for a battle the likes of which could spell disaster.

All that week Coach Kirk had spoken of how tough Marshfield would be. He reminded his players that Marshfield had always managed to play their best games against Rockland. He showed them the game film from the previous year, a game the Warriors had struggled to win 14-8. He even pulled out a tape from five years before when Marshfield had upset the Warriors 14-13.

He hoped that he had made it clear that if the Warriors did not play their best game against the Indians, the Warriors could be beaten. Coach Kirk's fears proved to be well-founded.

The Marshfield game started exactly as it was expected to. Big Dog Perez had taken a handoff on the second play from scrimmage and had dazzled the fans by zigzagging his way through the entire Marshfield team for a 74-yard touchdown. A bad snap from center caused the extra point to fail, but Rockland led 6-0 with less than three minutes gone in the game. The Warriors stopped the Indians cold in their next possession, and took over on their own forty-yard line. Led once again by the Big Dog, the Warriors drove 60 yards in just five plays, with Perez navigating the last thirty-two on another nifty run. This time, however, the shifty senior was hit hard as he crossed the goal line. He got up slowly and limped towards the sidelines. The Big Dog had sprained his ankle, and the trainer told Coach Kirk he would be lost for at least the rest of the game. With the loss of their star running back, the confidence seemed to go out of the Purple and White. The defense continued to shut down the Indians, but the offense had lost its spark, and it began to sputter.

Towards the end of the first half, facing a third and fifteen at its own thirty-five, the coach sent in a pass play designed to shake Danny free in a deep crossing pattern. Danny felt sure the play would work. He was a step or two faster than the safety, and he had watched both halfbacks support the run aggressively. He was certain he could get open. The play began well enough. Danny cut behind his wingback and sure enough, he was able to outrun the safety. He broke into the clear just beyond midfield.

Barry Lonigan, Rockland's junior quarterback, saw him and cocked his arm to throw. Just before he released the ball, the entire complexion of the game changed. The Marshfield defensive end, "the backside crasher" as he was referred to by Coach Kirk, broke past the usually reliable block of Jason Jones. The big fullback seldom missed his block, but he missed this one. The result was a crushing blindside tackle that caused the football to bounce in the direction of the Rockland goal line. A mad scramble followed, but the result was a recovery by the Marshfield noseguard on the Rockland twelve-yard line. The Warriors held for three plays, but on fourth and five at the Rockland seven, the Indians lined up in a shotgun formation and tried what appeared to be a power sweep to their right. Nearly the entire Warrior defense was there to meet the play. The problem was that there was no one left to cover Marshfield's quarterback, who, after pitching to his left halfback sweeping to the right, had managed to sneak uncovered into the corner of the Warrior's end zone. The Marshfield running back, after faking a sweep right, turned at the last instant and tossed a wobbly pass all the way across the field and into the waiting arms of the uncovered quarterback. The Marshfield fans went wild, and the Marshfield team was rejuvenated. They kicked the extra point, and with just over two minutes left in the first half, the score was Rockland 13, Marshfield 7. The Indians gambled on the ensuing kickoff.

Realizing that his team and the Marshfield fans were fired up, their coach called for an onsides kick.

The play worked to perfection. Marshfield recovered the ball around their own forty-five. On the first play from scrimmage the Warriors got caught in an all-out blitz, and the Marshfield halfback caught a screen pass with a convoy of blockers in front of him. The play resulted in a fifty-five-yard touchdown, and now bedlam rocked the stadium.

The first half ended with the Indians leading 14 to 13. In the Rockland locker room the players walked dazedly about or sat in stunned silence. Coach Kirk made his way into the room. The players who had been milling around sat down facing their coach. All of them waited silently for the explosion. It never came. Instead, Coach Kirk walked to the chalkboard. Quietly he diagrammed the Marshfield defense and explained that the reason the Indians had been so difficult to run against was because they had been jamming the line of scrimmage with nine defenders. He told his team that against any competent defense, even a great offense would find it difficult to defeat a nine-man front by running the football. If the Warriors were to win, they would need to pass and pass effectively. Coach Kirk told his team that they had receivers open on a number of pass plays, but that the quarterback would need time to get the ball to them. Consequently, he would be running only two-man and three-man pass patterns in the second half. He would be keeping the fullback and sometimes a halfback as well in the backfield to protect the quarterback. Coach Kirk spoke quietly and confidently to his team. He warned them that Marshfield would be fired up. He told them that every one of them would need to do exactly what he was told to do, and that if each of them played the way he was capable of playing, they could still win. The coach had managed to pull his team back together. They were ready to play their best football in the second half.

From the minute Marshfield received the second half kickoff, the Warriors saw they were in for the fight of their lives. Marshfield's young team was even more fired up than Rockland. They moved the football on the ground, and on fourth down their punter unleashed a tremendous kick that was downed at the Rockland two-yard line. Rockland was held on its first two running plays. On third and long, Barry Lonigan attempted to hit his tight end across the middle of the line with a short dump pass. He was hit just as he released the ball. His tight end made the catch and a first down at the seventeen. However, the veteran quarterback went down on the play, and went down hard. A few minutes later he was helped to his feet by both the trainer and the team doctor. He walked off the field under his own power, but he had thrown his last pass for the night. He had suffered a separated shoulder on his right side—his throwing side. There was no way of knowing how soon he would be able to return, or if he would be able to play out the season.

CHAPTER 15

How Football Legends Are Made

The Marshfield fans applauded the injured Warrior QB, but now the stands were rocking. They were beginning to sense a major upset, an upset that Marshfield would remember for years to come. Their enthusiasm spilled over to their team. Marshfield drove for a touchdown on its next possession, and their kicker boomed the extra point through the uprights to make it Marshfield 21, Rockland 13.

Marshfield kicked off and immediately showed that they had upset on their mind. Their defense pushed Rockland back. On fourth down and twelve a swarming punt rush nearly blocked the Warrior's punt. As it was, the kick trickled out of bounds a mere nineteen yards down the field.

The Indians drove the ball to the Rockland five where the now desperate Warrior defense stiffened. On fourth down the Marshfield kicker drilled a field goal through the heart of the goalposts and perhaps into the heart of the Warrior eleven.

When you have been around football long enough, you can almost smell an upset in the making. Coach Kirk had been around football his entire life. He smelled upset in the air. He didn't much like what he smelled.

The situation was becoming desperate. With just over a minute remaining in the third quarter, Rockland trailed a fired-up opponent by 11 points. They were without their star, Bo James and their starting running back, Big Dog Perez. Now they had lost their number one quarterback—maybe for the season. The Rockland defense was still solid, but it had been on the field much of the second half, and it was showing signs of tiring. The offense had apparently lost its leaders, its punch, and much of its confidence. Coach Kirk called a time-out and jogged out onto the field. He didn't like what he saw.

There was a look of panic in more than a few sets of eyes, and doubt was beginning to creep into even the most seasoned veterans' faces. Coach Kirk knew what he was looking for. Call it a hunch, or call it intuition. It was time for the wily veteran coach to show how legends were made. If Marshfield thought this game was over, they couldn't have been more wrong. What Coach Kirk was searching for he found in a most unlikely place—in the eyes of the youngest member of his team. And it was as if the old coach had the power to see inside his young player's heart.

There are many versions of what Coach Kirk said in the huddle in the short moment that followed. All of them are different and yet the same. However, every one of the versions is clear on how he began and how he ended. "Gentlemen, do not think for one minute that we are not going to win this game, because we are. Do not think for an instant that Marshfield has even the slightest chance of defeating us, because they do not. We are going to score on this very next play. Then our defense is going to hold.

We will not give them another inch. Our offense will get the ball back, and we will score again. We will from this point forward play the way Rockland High School has always played—like champions. If there is any one of you who has even the slightest doubt that what I am telling you is true, leave the field now, because there is no room for doubt on this football field."

A roar went up from inside the huddle. It began in the throat of the youngest member of that Rockland team and like a contagious bolt of lightening, shot through the minds and hearts of every player. As Coach Kirk left the huddle and headed for the sidelines, every player was determined that he would be a part of what each now believed would be a Warrior victory.

"100 Tight Right, Sprint Right, Fly-on two," said Bobby Williams. Every eye went to Danny. He felt that he needed to say something, but he had never before spoken in the varsity huddle. His face was a mask of stone. "Just get it close," he heard himself say to the quarterback. "I'll catch it."

The Marshfield defense still showed a nine-man front. After all, they had managed to shut down Rockland with it for three quarters, and now Rockland was without its starting quarterback.

The snap set the play in motion. Bobby Williams sprinted hard to his right. The motion back drew the attention of the weak safety. The strong safety rotated to the side of the wingback.

The halfback to the side of the sprint came up hard to defend. That left the inverted halfback to the weak side, Danny's side, to sprint back to cover the deep middle zone. Danny realized now that it wasn't really a man-to-man defense at all. It was a type of an inverted zone. No wonder they had been having problems most of the game. They had been reading the defense as a man-to-man with a 9-man front and it was actually an 8-man front with a 3-deep zone. Danny realized that if he attacked the defense the way the pass was drawn up, he would end up being covered by the middle safety. He adjusted his route accordingly and hoped Bobby Williams would see the change in time. Had it been the starting QB, Barry Lonigan, chances are he would not even have thrown the ball to Danny. Ironically, the fact that the former JV quarterback lacked the experience to pick out a secondary receiver worked to the Warriors' advantage. Bobby never took his eyes off of Danny. It's true that by looking right at him he tipped off the defender that that was where he planned to throw the ball, but it just didn't matter. Danny broke into the clear twenty yards down the field. Bobby Williams launched his throw a split second before being hit by the backside crasher. A groan went up from the Marshfield side of the field while a simultaneous cheer rose from the Rockland stands. Danny took the ball in stride at the Marshfield forty and out-raced the frantic Indian defenders into the end zone. The score was Marshfield 24, Rockland 19.

Everyone in the stadium realized that Rockland needed to go for two. Every eye was on the Rockland huddle as it broke and its players sprinted to the line of scrimmage. Every eye watched the Warriors line up in a tight wing to the right. They knew where the play was going—to the strong side of the field. Instead, the wingback went in motion from the right to the left. Bobby Williams rolled to his left. The Marshfield defense rotated their secondary quickly to the side of the motion back. There would be a host of defenders there to greet the Rockland QB. What they hadn't counted upon was Rockland's weak side end circling back to the side of the tight end. Danny took the toss from Bobby Williams and dashed for the far corner of the end zone. The play was a reverse, pure and simple. Marshfield recognized the skullduggery too late. Danny's run accounted for two additional points, and Rockland trailed by only a field goal.

Now the burden of winning fell squarely on the shoulders of the Warrior defense. They proved Coach Kirk a prophet by stuffing the Marshfield running game for three straight losses. On fourth and fourteen the Indians had to punt. Rockland took over in great field position at their own forty-three. They drove to the Marshfield seven where the determined Indians held. On fourth and goal from the seven and with the most reliable place kicker in the conference, Rags McKenzie, trotting out onto the field, it was beginning to look like there might be a good chance for an overtime contest. Rags lined up on the fourteen-yard line. A twenty-four-yard field goal was just a chip shot for Rags. The snap went to Bobby Williams. Rags swung his foot. The crowd gasped. He hadn't kicked the ball. Instead, Bobby Williams was looping the ball into the back of the end zone. And there, leaping high into the air and coming down with the ball clutched in his hands was "the kid who could."

CHAPTER 16

The Kid Who Could

In the newspapers the next day, Danny Cannon and Bobby Williams were singled out by Coach Kirk for their ability to come through in the clutch. Together with his defense, he was more pleased with the offensive performance of this JV tandem than with any other aspect of the game. Coach Kirk was quoted as saying that he felt his squad had learned a valuable lesson in Saturday's game, a lesson that he hoped all of them would apply to their lives. They had learned that you must never allow yourself to give up. They had handled adversity and internal as well as external pressure. They had learned the value of teamwork, because only by pulling together had they reached their common goal.

John Kirk praised Marshfield for what he called a "valiant effort" and went so far as to say that the Indians had deserved to win, perhaps even more than the Warriors. Both teams, he said, had given it their all. Only a few breaks and a few key plays separated the teams. John Kirk called the game a confirmation of the need to play football with the heart. He was convinced that the victory would help his team, and the defeat would make Marshfield a better team as well.

Danny was christened "The Kid Who Could." Fans, the press, and most of his teammates heralded Danny as the next Bo James. Bo James himself hugged him at the end of the game. "You got game, kid. You sure do have game," he told the flattered freshman.

Even Big Dog Perez begrudgingly praised Danny saying: "You can play on my team any day. You don't do it as good as the Big Dog do it, but you get the job done. And, that what matters, Little Dog. The Big Dog be glad you on his side."

The experience they picked up in the Marshfield game taught the Purple and White a lesson. Despite having lost several key performers, the Warriors trounced Springridge (27-0) and Juniper Falls (35-7) on successive weeks. They got the Big Dog back against the Glasgow Highlanders, and he contributed three touchdowns and close to two hundred yards in rushing in a 42-16 victory. The Warriors extended their record to 7-0 and were on a collision course with the undefeated Valley West Pioneers. However, they still needed to get by a mediocre Cedarbrook squad and the once beaten Whitehall Grenadiers, if the long-awaited showdown were to be for the league championship.

Danny Cannon had become an integral part of the Warriors offensive arsenal. He was averaging 6.5 catches and just over eighteen yards per catch for the season. In addition, he had caught seven touchdown passes and three two-point conversions. Add to that the touchdown that he had scored on an interception return, and Danny had a very impressive set of statistics.

Opposing coaches became aware of Danny's offensive contributions, and they began to cover him with their better secondary personnel; in some situations they even double covered him. As a result, Coach Kirk had often used Danny as a decoy, and had set up several plays in which Danny's assignment was to clear an area by running his pass route away from where the ball would eventually be thrown. Coach Kirk was as impressed with Danny's unselfish attitude as he was with his ability to make clutch catches, and he made his feelings known to the press and to college scouts. Danny was as happy as he could ever remember being. However, adversity suddenly came in an unexpected form.

CHAPTER 17

Stranger in the Stands

Nancy Cannon's life had long revolved around her son. For the last fourteen years he had come first, and she had never given a thought as to whether or not that was the way things ought to be. At times she had had to be both mother and father. More than once she felt thankful that Red was there to help the boy and to be the father figure that every boy so badly needed in his life. Still, even Red could not always fill the void left by Jeffrey Cannon.

Nancy never considered her ex-husband bad. She didn't hate him, even though it would have been natural and even understandable for her to feel that way. She had never allowed bitterness to consume her, though sometimes she resented Jeff Cannon's spinelessness and his unwillingness to become involved with their son. She was a remarkable woman, and Danny showed his appreciation by doing what he knew was right.

One night after practice, Danny noticed a solitary figure sitting in the bleachers. He appeared to be adjusting a pair of binoculars. Danny wouldn't have found this strange, but the man appeared to be looking directly at him and nobody else. Danny debated walking over to him, but the man apparently sensed that Danny was aware of being watched, and he quickly made his way down the stadium's exit ramp and out the gate.

That evening at dinner Danny mentioned the incident to his mother. She frowned, appeared to be in deep thought for a moment or two, and then sort of shrugged and told her son not to worry. She said that such things were the price of fame, and, after all, he was becoming quite a celebrity. Danny reddened almost imperceptibly, but then turned the issue into a joke. "You're right," he said. "It was probably just that feature writer from *Sports Illustrated* who keeps wanting to do a story about me."

"Oh, too bad," Nancy Cannon teased, "I was hoping it was ESPN. Someone said that they pay more for their features, and we could use the money."

Mother and son shared the laugh, but she did not forget the incident. She didn't like it. It filled her with foreboding and made her wish she knew where Danny's father was. It would be so like him to do something stupid to ruin her son's happiness. She was working herself up into a major fret when the phone rang. It was Steve Mitman. He was in town to see Bo James, and he wanted to know if he could have his rain check on that dinner he was promised. Although the unexpected call caught Nancy off guard, she managed to tell Steve there was "no expiration date" on his rain check. Her answer made him smile.

"Let's make it tomorrow night," he said. "But it will be my treat, and Danny's invited too. I'll pick the two of you up around eight."

Nancy happily agreed, then wished she had asked Steve about what would be appropriate dress. She almost called him back but decided against it. She didn't want to sound too eager. Still, her heart was beating a bit faster, and she chided herself for acting like a silly schoolgirl. *After all, she reminded herself, It isn't like this is a real date. It's just dinner. My son is going with us. It's not really a date at all.*

No matter how she struggled to convince herself, she realized that there was a part of her that wanted to at least think that this really was a date. Her desire made her blush, but it made her happy too. She hadn't dated for a very long time. She wasn't even sure how she was supposed to act. What if he held her hand? Surely he wouldn't try to kiss her with Danny along. She tried to remember her last date with Steve Mitman, but it had been so long ago that she just couldn't. Finally she gave up trying to remember.

That night she dreamed of a time long ago. She was at her prom, was wearing a gown and a beautiful corsage. Her date was gazing into her eyes. He was about to kiss her. She was about to let him, when suddenly she realized it wasn't Steve Mitman; it was Jeffrey Cannon, and he wasn't taking no for an answer. Nancy Cannon awoke. She didn't get back to sleep for a long time.

At breakfast the next morning, Nancy told Danny they had a dinner engagement with Steve. She was startled when Danny said that he wouldn't be able to go. He mumbled something about needing to study for a science test. Nancy had never anticipated the possibility that Danny might not want to go to dinner with her and an escort. She was certain that Danny had liked Steve as much as Steve had liked Danny. His decision to pass up the invitation puzzled her. She decided to see if her father could shed some light on the unexpected turn of events. She called him the minute Danny left for school.

"Red" was no authority on women. What he knew about dating wouldn't fill a small thimble, but he knew his grandson and he understood how he thought. When his daughter had explained the turn of events, it took old Red less than a minute to figure out what was going on. Chuckling to himself, Red told his daughter "You've got a great kid there."

"I know that," she said, "But why doesn't he want to go out to dinner with Steve and me?"

"I should think a smart girl like you could have figured that out for herself. It's not that he doesn't *want* to go. It's that he doesn't want to blow a good thing for you. Danny's afraid that if he goes out with the two of you, it won't be much of a date. Evidently he really likes Steve. He must think you do too. He wants you to have a chance to go out without having to drag your fourteen- year-old son along with you. I'd say that makes him smart as well as considerate.

Nancy sat open-mouthed. "That thought never so much as crossed my mind," she said.

"Well, it's the first thought that crossed mine," said Red. "Any man would know that Steve just invited Danny to be polite."

Nancy had to admit that her father's analysis of the situation made perfect sense, but she needed to be sure. She decided to call Steve Mitman and tell him that Danny wouldn't be able to go to dinner with the two of them. She wanted to check his reaction. She called the hotel where he was staying. He was out, so she left a message at the desk to call her as soon as he got back in.

Around four that afternoon, Steve called her at work. She explained the situation.

"No need to apologize to me," he said. "School has to come first. I'd still like to buy you dinner if you can make it," he added.

"That would be fine," she said. "By the way, where are we going?"

"Saint Anthony's Youth Center," Steve said "I'm the featured speaker."

A smile spread across Nancy's face. *How very unromantic,* she thought to herself. *I should have known.*

Secretly she felt a bit relieved. At least she now knew what to wear. She'd been to enough of these dinners to know. No need to worry about being kissed. If Steve so much as gave her a peck on the cheek at the end of the night she'd be surprised. *Football coaches!* she thought to herself. *Their idea of a date is to scout the next team on*

the schedule while sharing the binoculars with their wives.
Still, the thought of being escorted to dinner by a very
handsome old beau did make her pulse quicken.

○   ○   ○

It was nearly midnight when Steve finally dropped Nancy
off at her front door. She had to admit, it had been a
wonderful date. The dinner, typical banquet affair of roast
turkey, steamship beef, and baked ham platters with mashed
potatoes, filling, and big steaming bowls of corn was tasty
but nothing special. Likewise the small appetizers of
canned fruit cocktail left much to be desired. That didn't
matter much, however. Steve's talk had been terrific. His
audience had listened in rapt attention as he explained the
lessons about life that football teaches those who play it.
She realized that what he said was true, and the way he
said it made her realize that he was the kind of man she
would want her child to have for a coach. What was more,
she realized that this was the kind of man she should have
chosen to be the father of her son.

After dinner, Steve chose to stick around to meet with
several of the young men and to talk with their parents
about the opportunities the University of Michigan offered
to its graduates. It was a few minutes after ten when Steve
finally escorted Nancy to his car. They drove to the
Colonial Diner and spent the next two hours talking about
old times. They shared their plans for the future, and
complimented one another on how little they had changed
over the years. Nancy laughed and accused Steve of having
spent too much time kissing the Blarney stone.

It was, Nancy decided, the fastest two hours she had ever spent with anyone. When Steve finally left her at her front door after kissing her good night, she decided she owed her son a huge chocolate malted, maybe two. It was the least she could do for his thoughtfulness. There was no doubt in Nancy Cannon's mind that she was falling in love.

CHAPTER 18

On a Collision Course

That Saturday Rockland handled Cedarbrook as easily as expected. The final score was Rockland 49, Cedarbrook 12. It had been what some might term "a real laugher."

Danny had caught two touchdown passes, one of twelve yards, and the second a forty-one yarder that was a thing of beauty. He had leap high between two defenders in the middle of the field, caught the ball on his fingertips, come down with it, and then zigzagged his way through three more would-be tacklers without being hit solidly by any one of them.

The word was that Valley West had beaten Whitehall in overtime, eliminating them from any chance of even sharing the championship. Still, the score, Valley West 27, Whitehall 24, indicated how closely matched the two teams had been. If Rockland were to win the championship, they would need to do it the old fashioned way—they'd need to earn it.

The first two months of school had come and gone. Danny was doing well in most of his classes. He was struggling a little in Algebra, but Mr. Dimmick, a no-nonsense former navy commander, was willing to devote extra time to helping him, so he often spent his lunchtime in the math room working on algebra problems under the old teacher's scrutiny. Danny appreciated the extra time his algebra teacher spent with him. Although he had to budget his time so tightly that he had little for anything except football and his studies, Danny was happy with his life. The thing that bothered him, though, was that on some days he would have to cut back on the time he spent lifting weights. He felt guilty when this happened, but he realized that there were always going to be difficult choices that would have to be made if he hoped to accomplish his goals.

At home, Nancy noticed a new maturity in Danny. She was proud of him, not just because he was doing well both on the football field and in the classroom, but because he was making good choices in his life. She had always feared that perhaps she was being unfair to her son by not remarrying, but she no longer felt guilty about the choices she had made in her own life. Danny was a fine young man, a son who would make any parent proud.

The Monday before the Whitehall game, Danny once again spotted the man watching him through binoculars. He had mentioned the previous incident to Bo James who, when he wasn't in the trainer's room rehabilitating his left knee, or jogging the cinder track in his team sweatsuit, could be found in the back of the team's huddle helping his replacement learn his assignments on each play. The injured star had taken a personal interest in the athletic Danny, and in addition to encouraging him on the football field, had been like a big brother to him when Danny needed to discuss a personal problem. Despite his debilitating knee injury, the scouts continued to pursue Bo James. He had hoped to be ready for the Whitehall game, but both the team doctor and Coach Kirk were concerned that that would be unwise. They didn't want to jeopardize his future by bringing him back too soon and risking permanent damage to his knee. And so, as the team ran through their game plan, Bo James remained in the back of the huddle stretching his leg muscles, and yelling encouragement to his teammates.

After the starting team had run a play and jogged back to the huddle, Danny made it a point to stand beside Bo James and call Bo's attention to the man in the stands. Bo thought that it might be a Whitehall scout, and decided to go investigate. Casually he began to jog the cinder track, but when he had circled the oval to the point of being on the far side of the track and just twenty or thirty yards from the stands, he angled off of the cinders and over toward the bleachers. Danny watched the team captain's confrontation with the man. He noted that the man had put his binoculars back in their case and seemed to be speaking earnestly. The conversation lasted several minutes, after which Bo jogged the rest of the way around the track and returned to the huddle. Danny had run a handful of plays from the time his friend had gone on his discovery mission till the time he returned. He was bursting with curiosity to find out what Bo had learned, but Coach Kirk intensified the pace of the workout, and there was no time to ask Bo anything. Bo apparently found no pressing need to share his information, so, Danny had to wait for what seemed like forever to learn what his friend had discovered.

Immediately after his wind sprints, Danny sought Bo. But the senior had left the field to work on strengthening his knee. Danny showered quickly then rushed to the trainer's room. Bo was in the adjacent weight room sitting at the leg press machine, diligently straining to strengthen his knee.

Danny approached in a hurry to learn what Bo had found out.

"What did you find out—about that guy with the binoculars?" Danny asked Bo James.

"Not too much," Bo replied. "Just that he was a Rockland fan, not a Whitehall scout."

"Is that all?" asked Danny.

"Yeah, that's all. Oh, one other thing. He said that his name is Jeffrey Cannon, and he's your father."

Danny's jaw dropped a foot. He stood there. Speechless.

"My fa-father?" he began. "He said he was *my* father?"

"That's what he said. Oh yeah. He also said to tell you he'd be coming by to see you soon."

Stunned by the turn of events, Danny was frozen, not quite believing what he had just heard. What could his father be doing in the bleachers with a pair of binoculars? Why would he tell Bo James that he would be seeing Danny soon? Why did he have to turn up now and here?

Danny felt a mixture of fear and anger welling up inside. He was afraid that his father would somehow ruin everything. What his father might do was unknown, but he was afraid that his father's appearance now, when things were going so well for both his mother and him, would change both of their lives, and the change would not be for the better.

Gradually Danny's fear subsided, and he grew angry. *What right does this man, this man who claims to be my father, have to turn up after all these years? How dare he think that it is acceptable to suddenly appear out of nowhere and announce that he is my father?* The more Danny thought about it, the madder he became. It wasn't like him to get so angry, but Danny suddenly hated the man who had decided to appear after all these years of neglect. Inside, Danny felt as if his stomach was doing flip-flops. He felt all mixed up, and the churning sensation wasn't going away.

Bo James asked Danny if something was wrong. Danny desperately wanted to tell him yes. He wanted to tell him his whole world had just been turned upside-down. He wanted to tell him how he felt. He wanted to tell him everything. Instead, he just shook his head. "No," he said. "Everything is just great." Then Danny turned and abruptly left the room.

When he got home, his mother was still at work. She had left a note telling Danny that she'd be working a little late, but that she'd be home by 7:00, and she'd be bringing dinner with her. In the meantime, he was to eat a piece of fruit or have some orange juice, just something to take the edge off, because he'd need to save his appetite for what she was bringing.

Danny didn't feel hungry anyway. The last thing he felt like doing was eating. He didn't feel much like studying either. He didn't even feel like lifting weights. Instead he flipped on the TV, something he used to do all the time, but something he hadn't done in months. He was in the midst of watching some inane game show when the phone rang. He felt almost afraid to answer it. Not afraid in the sense of feeling fear, but afraid that it might be his father calling, and he wouldn't know what to say to him. He considered letting the machine answer the call, but decided that that would be cowardly. He picked it up on the third ring. It was his grandfather. Relief flooded over Danny. His grandfather would know what to do. He always did.

Minutes later, Danny spilled the whole story. All the while he spoke, Red said nothing. Now, as Danny grew silent, his grandfather explained what needed to be done. He told Danny not to worry, and not to bother his mother by telling her about his father's return, at least not just yet. He told Danny that he would meet with his father and find out what he wanted. "Let me handle everything. If I need your help, I'll let you know," Red said. Danny was relieved. He trusted Red. His grandfather had always known what to do whenever there was a problem and Danny had no reason to doubt his grandfather's ability to handle this problem too.

Already Danny felt relieved, as if a boulder had been rolled off of his chest. Just as he hung up the phone, his mother came through the front door. In her arms was a bucket of fried chicken with all the trimmings. Suddenly Danny felt his appetite return.

CHAPTER 19

Bad News—Good News

The Friday before the Whitehall game, Coach Kirk announced to the team that Bo James had been cleared to play the following week against Valley West, but that they would need to face Whitehall without him.

There was an undercurrent of whispers, and then a general humming of voices, followed by a tremendous shout as if a dam had burst. The championship, at one time so distant, now seemed within reach. The pent-up anxieties of the varsity squad had finally burst out. And each player allowed himself to ease up just a bit, which spelled disaster. When the dust cleared from the field at Whitehall stadium the next night, the scoreboard read: Rockland 24, Whitehall 27. The bus ride home was agony. Big Dog Perez didn't have to endure it. He had been carried off the field to the hospital with a broken ankle just before the end of the first half, with Rockland clinging to a 21 to 17 lead. With the Big Dog out of the game, Whitehall used double coverage on Danny in passing situations. The result was that Danny, who had caught five passes for more than a hundred yards and one touchdown in the first half, was limited to one reception for nine yards in the second half. The Whitehall defense also shut down Rockland's depleted running game. They allowed Rockland just thirty-three yards on the ground. A Rags McKenzie field goal brought the Warriors back from a 24 to 21 deficit to a 24 to 24 tie with two minutes remaining in the game. But the Whitehall kickoff return man shook free on the following kickoff, and only a desperation tackle by Skeeter Simms prevented him from going all the way. Instead Whitehall had the ball first and goal at the four-yard line with two minutes left to play. As it was, Rockland, led by Ross Tanner and Tank Harmon made a ferocious goal line stand. But with less than twenty seconds to go, and the ball resting on the Rockland seven-yard line, Whitehall sent in its field goal unit. Their soccer-style kicker managed to drill the ball between the desperate arms of a leaping Ross Tanner, and Whitehall led 27 to 24 with twelve seconds left and Rockland out of timeouts. When Whitehall squib-kicked the next kickoff and tackled Scooter McPeak at midfield, time ran out. Now the best Rockland could hope for was a tie for the league title if they could manage to defeat unbeaten Valley West the following Saturday.

A heavy gloom filled the Rockland bus as it drove through the Pennsylvania mountains in the dark.

Red Evans was waiting at the side entrance to the locker room when the Rockland bus pulled in. He was evidently in a hurry for the bus to unload its tired cargo. As the door opened and Coach Kirk stepped down, Danny's grandfather took the coach aside and began gesturing and talking excitedly. A short time after, the team captains told the squad that they were to meet in the team room as soon as they hung up their pads. Danny was surprised that his grandfather was standing beside the coach. Coach Kirk stood in front of the squad and allowed the buzzing to die down before he spoke.

"I know it's late," he said, "But Mr. Evans has been thoughtful enough to bring us some interesting news. I'm going to let him address you."

His grandfather stepped up and looked directly at the expectant team.

"I happened to be listening to the radio on my way home from the game tonight. It seems we weren't the only team to have the air let out of our balloon. Marshfield just upset Valley West 17 to 14, in overtime. That means that the two teams playing for the championship next week will each have one loss. That's you, and Valley West!"

Coach Kirk stepped to the front. "Thanks for the good news, Red," he said. "It's not often in life that you get this kind of a second chance. Gentlemen, you need to get home and get some sleep. The time to start preparing to win that championship is now."

Cheers erupted. The team got the message. It was not really as good as winning, but was a whole lot better than needing to win again just to gain a tie.

On the way home, Red told Danny that he had met with Jeff Cannon. He was getting remarried, and wanted both Danny and Nancy to know that he hoped to start his new life a wiser man. He was proud of Danny and wanted to visit him in person, but he knew Nancy wouldn't approve. Instead, he would continue to watch Danny from a distance, as he had been doing. It would be best for both of them.

At eighteen, Danny could choose whether or not he wanted to meet face-to-face. His mother was "doing a great job of raising the kid", he said.

That was about all there was to it, except Jeffrey had left a $200.00 check for Nancy to be given to her right after Thanksgiving. It was postdated for December 1st.

Danny knew his mother. He could tell how she felt by the way she smiled, or tried to smile. He understood her ups and downs, her likes and her dislikes. He loved her for what she was and for what she was not. He would have done anything for her. Sometimes he worried about her, and wondered if she could ever be really happy. He seldom told his mother his feelings about anything, but he tried to please her and make her life easier in any way that he could. The two of them had faced life's hardships together. Aside from Red, they expected no help from anyone. Danny didn't mind so much for himself, but there were times when he worried that his mother wouldn't be able to handle the daily pressures, the bills, the constant financial obligations that are a part of being a single parent.

His fears were well founded, but Nancy Cannon never showed that she felt sorry for herself. Until recently, she had been so busy working and raising a child, she hadn't time to realize she'd been neglecting her social life. Only since Steve Mitman entered her life again had she begun to think about how warm and wonderful it was to be in love. For a man such as Steve Mitman, she was willing to take the risk of having her heart broken, again.

Steve Mitman, never married, had been searching for something that he couldn't explain. He derived fulfillment from his job, and he had no problem finding companionship when that is what he craved. However, deep inside there was a void. He couldn't put it into words—not even for himself. It was like some long-ago echo that faded but wouldn't be totally silent. When he was with Nancy Cannon, he felt whole. When he was with both Nancy and Danny, he felt needed and wanted. He wasn't sure what he planned to do about his feelings, but he knew he didn't want to lose Nancy again. He knew he could love the boy as if he were his own. He was confident that Nancy felt the same way about him as he did about her. He hoped that Danny would allow him to become part of his life as well as his mother's. He planned to find out.

○ ○ ○

Rockland's preparation for the Valley West game was like nothing Danny ever experienced. Coach Kirk and his staff were methodical and meticulous. They refused to leave a single detail to chance. The scouting report they passed out was sixteen pages long. It contained every bit of information that could make even a shred of difference in the upcoming game. It explained West's hash-mark tendencies, their formation tendencies, their down and distance tendencies, their favorite pass patterns, their favorite running plays. He listed their key personnel together with a strength and weakness profile on each player. And there was more.

The strengths and weaknesses of the defenses used by West were examined, analyzed, scrutinized, and dissected. The Rockland game plan was drawn up accordingly. Coach Kirk believed firmly that his teams might sometimes be out-scored, occasionally out-played, but they would never be out-hustled, out-conditioned, or out-prepared. The veteran coach lived by his principles.

When game day finally arrived, the Rockland Warriors felt confident that they were as well prepared as any high school team could ever be. Moreover, with Bo James back in the starting lineup for the Purple and White, the Warriors felt confident that they would win. It was still several hours till opening kickoff, but Rockland High School was as ready as any Rockland football team had ever been. Coach Wilson had a saying that he liked to share with anyone in earshot just before game time: "The hay is in the barn." It meant that the team was as well prepared as it could possibly be; everything and everyone was ready. Bring on the storm.

The storm came in the form of a punishing Valley West ground attack. The storm came in the form of a huge offensive line and a bruising fullback. The storm came in the form of a tailback who was as hard to tackle as a Halloween shadow. Valley West High School thundered in.

West took the opening kickoff and marched the length of the field in fifteen black-and-blue-tinged plays. First it was a straight dive to the two hundred thirty-pound fullback for five yards. Then the tailback followed his

100

Godzilla-sized lead-blocker and his herd of dinosaur-like linemen in an off-tackle power play for another eight yards. The opening drive was as devastating as Sherman's March to the Sea.

When the fullback finally drove deep into the end zone, the Rockland defenders blinked in horror and disbelief. He had carried three Rockland tacklers across the goal line with him, and the entire Rockland defensive team lay strewn about as if on some battlefield. With nearly nine minutes gone in the first quarter, Rockland trailed 7 to 0, and their offense had not yet touched the football.

Valley West kicked the ball deep into the Rockland end zone. From there it was made ready for play at the twenty. On first down, Bo James took the ball deep in his backfield where he was immediately swarmed by a host of tacklers. He hadn't a chance to get started. The powerful running back had shaken off two tacklers, but only a super effort enabled him to get back to the line of scrimmage. On second and ten, Bobby Williams dropped back to throw. The way the defenders blasted through the offensive line, it looked like a perfect screen pass had been set up, but unfortunately a screen pass hadn't been called. The result was a quarterback sack and a six-yard loss. On third and sixteen, a blitzing West linebacker hit Williams as he extended the football toward Bo James on what was to have been a draw play. The fumble rolled to the Rockland seven where a big Valley West defensive end pounced on the pigskin, giving his team a first and goal to go just seven yards from pay dirt. Two plays later, Valley West led 13 to 0 and the PAT was a mere formality. The score quickly read Valley West 14, Rockland 0.

Rockland received the kickoff for the second time in the first quarter, trailing 14 to 0.

After three straight handoffs to Bo James netted only four yards, Rockland punted. It took Valley West just eight plays to cover fifty-seven yards and score their third touchdown of the first quarter. The extra point was good once again, and the score now was 21 to 0.

Even the most loyal and optimistic Warrior rooters sat in stunned disbelief. Coach Kirk stood frowning at his elaborate game charts. Nothing had gone according to plan. He called his coaches to him. What was happening? What was Valley West doing, and why wasn't his team handling it? He sought the opinion of first one coach and then the next. From his coaches in the press box he learned that, offensively, West was running almost exclusively from a power-I formation. So far they had not even attempted a pass. Coach Kirk decided to invert his secondary as Marshfield had done against West. That would leave the Warriors a bit susceptible to the pass, but it would force Valley West to block a nine-man front, and it would jam the middle effectively. The second adjustment made by Coach Kirk stunned even his own staff. Since Valley West had set up its defense exclusively to stop Bo James, Rockland would shift James back to where he could do them the most good—at inside linebacker on defense. In place of Bo James on offense they would insert a blocking back to give Bobby Williams a bit more time. In addition, since West was blitzing their inside linebackers on nearly every play, the quarterback would shorten his number of steps from nine to five on the drop-back passes. He would sprint to the wingback side of the formation, and the offensive line would use sprint-out blocking principles and a basic type of area blocking. Williams would look to throw the ball down the field to any of the three receivers who would be running pass patterns. The results were immediate and effective. With Bo James out of the game, West's defensive scheme backfired. It left them attempting to cover three "quick" receivers with two deep defenders. Their only real hope was to get to the Warrior quarterback before he could get the ball off. However, with an extra receiver being kept in to block, the blitzing linebacker found himself unable to get to the QB, and with the quarterback releasing the ball sooner, the West defenders needed to call a time out.

In the meantime Bobby Williams had connected on six consecutive pass plays, the last being a gem that Danny had pulled down at the West five-yard line. On the first play from the five, Williams sprinted to his right, tucked the ball under his arm, and followed his fullback into the end zone. Rags McKenzie booted the PAT, and the scoreboard read Valley West 21, Rockland 7.

The Big Red Machine took the ensuing kickoff at its five and returned it to its own thirty. On the first snap from scrimmage, the Valley tailback took the handoff behind his behemoth line only to be cut down by a human buzz saw at the line of scrimmage. Mr. tailback, meet Mr. Bo James—Mr. tailback, meet Mr. turf.

On two more successive plunges into the line, Bo James and company drove Valley West five yards backward. The Big Red Machine had not only stalled, they had been put in reverse. The Rockland stands came alive. First they cheered, then they exploded. Bo James had switched from offense to defense. The impact had been both sudden and dramatic. The Rockland defense had become more than an immovable object, it had become a surging wave, driving the seemingly unstoppable West juggernaut back towards its own goal line.

And now the Rockland offense hit its stride. No longer was it the churning and relentless ground game led by its All-State running back, Bo James. Instead it had become an aerial circus, led by a strong-armed and fearless (former JV) quarterback, Bobby Williams, and a freshman wide receiver, Danny Cannon.

The Warriors drove for their second touchdown with little more than half a minute left in the second quarter. No longer able to employ double coverage on Danny, the Big Red attempted to single cover him with their best defensive back. As Bobby Williams would be quoted as saying in the newspaper the next day "Not bloody likely!"

Danny was too fast and too slick. His routes were too precise, and his cuts too sharp.

It was almost as if he and Bobby Williams shared the same mind. When the defender played too tightly, Danny would fly by him, posing a scoring threat on every play. When the defender gave him too much cushion, Danny would hook or curl in front of him. When the defender played inside of him, Danny would break sharply to the sideline where he'd plant his feet and stop on a dime. Williams would deliver the strike, and leave the defender wondering what he had done wrong. If the defender played Danny on his outside shoulder, Danny would cut crisply across the middle of the field behind the Valley linebackers and catch the ball before the bewildered headhunters could furnish any help.

Danny caught his ninth pass of the first half in the far corner of the end zone. It was what he and Bobby had dubbed their "Led Zeppelin." It was sort of a lob into the corner of the end zone, too high to be caught by the defensive back, but thrown softly enough for Danny to position his body like a basketball rebounder and simply leap up and take it away from the defender. The play worked to perfection. Rockland left the field at halftime trailing 21 to 14, but from the reaction of the crowd as well as the Warriors, you'd have thought the scoreboard read Rockland 21, Valley West 14.

During the halftime break, Coach Kirk and his staff made a few more minor adjustments, but then he surprised everyone by explaining that they would start the second half with Bo James in the offensive backfield and the game plan would be to run the football, at least for the first series. That, he explained, was to keep West off balance, for he knew that they were undoubtedly making some frantic adjustments of their own even as he spoke. When West went back to its nine-man front, as it would quickly be forced to do, Rockland would switch back to its passing attack with one major change: Bo James would stay in to block for Bobby Williams and act as a threat to run the draw.

Before they went back onto the field, Coach Kirk called his team together. He asked them to look into the faces of their teammates. He told them to think about how hard each of them had worked to get to where they were. He told them to make a promise. The promise was, to their teammates and to themselves. The promise was when they came back into that locker room at the end of the game, to be able to look each of their teammates squarely in the eye and say from the heart: "I gave it all that I had. I did my very best for you." And then to walk over to the mirror and look squarely into it and say, "I did my very best. I played as hard as I could on every single play."

Every Rockland player made that promise. Every Rockland player made a commitment in that locker room.

Rockland took possession of the football at its own twenty-yard line after the second half kickoff soared into the end zone. On the first play from scrimmage, Bobby Williams dropped back as if to pass. He handed the ball instead deep in the backfield to Bo James. Valley West had dropped six defenders and rushed only its front five. They were caught completely flat-footed. The last thing they had expected was a draw. The last player they expected to see carrying the ball was Bo James. But when

Rockland opened the corral gate, out stepped their big horse, their thoroughbred, and Valley West could only hope to contain him. They managed to pull the "horse" down, but not before he had picked up considerable yardage—twenty-seven to be exact.

On first down, Rockland made no bones about where the ball was going. Bobby Williams turned on his left foot and handed the ball to a slashing Bo James. Eighteen yards later, it was again first and ten, but now it was from the Valley West twenty-five-yard line. Two more handoffs to Bo James, and Rockland trailed by a single point: 21 to 20. Reliable Rags McKenzie once more came through with a clutch kick, and the score was tied 21 to 21.

Valley West received, and after returning the kickoff to its own forty-three-yard line, it began its own methodical march to a score. As the third quarter drew to a close, West had opened up a 28 to 21 lead. The game had become a wide-open affair with both coaches throwing caution to the wind. Valley West continued to try to wear down Rockland with its brutal running game, but now they cleverly mixed in play-action passes, and Rockland had its hands full. On the other side of the line of scrimmage, Rockland had become "Air Kirk" with some occasional draw plays and counter traps featuring Bo James as an ever-present threat to run the football. Coach Kirk continued to count on the talent as well as the endurance of his star, Bo James, in an attempt to contain the Valley West offensive machine.

Neither the coach, nor Bo himsel,f had expected Rockland's star to need to go both ways, but Bo was giving it his all on both sides of the line of scrimmage. Even the most optimistic Rockland fan could see that it was only a matter of time till Bo dropped from sheer exhaustion, but meanwhile he continued to be a human dynamo, and he remained Rockland's beacon of hope in a sea of Valley West red.

Danny no longer played like a freshman. He had grown up during the course of a season. Now, here he was in his tenth varsity football game, and although no one had said so, he knew that it would be up to him to make a major contribution on offense if Rockland were to have any real chance of beating the physically stronger Valley West eleven.

Danny made use of every physical skill he possessed to make himself an offensive threat on every play. However, Danny's greatest asset wasn't his physical skill at all; it was his mental awareness together with his pure athletic instincts. As the game wore on, he became more and more familiar with the defensive techniques used by the Valley West defenders. He knew that West's strong safety, a well-built athlete who stood about six-one and weighed perhaps a hundred and ninety-five pounds, was very aggressive. He liked to cover Danny tightly when West went man-to-man. He would attempt to jam Danny hard at the line of scrimmage and try to prevent him from making a clean release into the pass pattern. Another thing Danny noticed was that when Valley West played a zone, the same strong safety came up hard at the first hint of a run, and he gave outstanding support to the defensive ends and linebackers on his side of the field. Danny had a tough time blocking him, but he was certain he could beat him on a deep route when the strong safety was forced to cover Danny man to man. Danny also felt certain that this defender was vulnerable to a play-action pass, and he relayed this information to his quarterback. When the time was right, Danny was sure he would be able to find a way to beat this formidable defender deep.

The free safety was another story. He was a taller, rangier athlete with outstanding speed. At about six-three and a hundred and eighty-five pounds, he was not much stronger than Danny, but he was a few steps faster. He wasn't as effective at stopping the run as the strong safety, but he covered a lot of ground, and really flew to the ball when it was in the air. Any pass thrown deep had better not be thrown too softly, or the free safety would be likely to pick it off. Danny shared this information with Bobby Williams as well. Likewise, at halftime, Danny made Coach Kirk aware of what he had seen. The coach thanked him and said that this was good to know, and that he would file it away in his mental notebook for future use.

No sooner had Valley West regained the lead than Rockland began another offensive drive of its own. They returned the Valley West kickoff to their own twenty-eight-yard line. Coach Kirk would either send the plays in with an offensive lineman, or use hand signals to inform his young quarterback of what he wanted to call next.

Coach Kirk called three straight running plays. The first was an inside counter that featured both the left guard and left tackle pulling to their right and leading Bo James on a wide slant that went between the right tackle and right end. The play was run from a wing right formation with the two remaining halfbacks split.

They were aligned so that their noses were directly behind the outside leg of the offensive guard on their sides of the football. Both the center and the right guard would seal block to their left. The tight end on the left would seal to his right for the pulling tackle. The quarterback would fake the ball to the right halfback who would run a dive over his right guard, and cause both the onside linebacker and nose-guard, as well as the onside defensive tackle to react to his fake. Meanwhile, the left guard pulled to his right and looked to block the first man beyond the offensive right tackle. Right behind him came the left tackle. When he saw the guard in front of him begin his block, he immediately dropped his left arm toward the ground to direct his left shoulder into the off-tackle hole. From there, his assignment was simple: attack the first opposite-colored jersey to show up. While this was happening, Bo James took a hard jab step to his left to make the play look as if it were going in that direction. Instead, he would then pivot on his left foot and cut hard to his right. He would follow his pulling left tackle into the hole that the guard and tackle were creating. Bo James loved this play and often broke it for a touchdown, or at least for a long gain. This time was no exception. Bo took the handoff and cut into the hole. The two deep safeties finally forced him out-of-bounds at the Valley West forty-three-yard line. It had been good for a gain of twenty-nine yards. On the next play, Bo slammed straight ahead for six yards, and then he picked up the first down by gaining seven more on a toss sweep to his left.

With the ball at the Valley West sixteen, West went into a nine-man front with both of their safeties up tight. On first down, Coach Kirk called for a power play to the right. West wasn't buying it. The entire left side of their defensive line, together with the strong safety and onside linebacker, slammed the door in Bo's face after he had fought for a yard. Facing the same nine-man front, Coach Kirk signaled in a play-action pass. Bo James did his bit. He faked a dive into the line of scrimmage and was met by a host of Valley West defenders. Unfortunately for them, Bobby Williams had neatly hidden the ball on his hip, and after the fake to James, he had rolled to his left. The strong safety bit. The free safety scrambled to pick up Danny who had faked a seal block on the inside linebacker and was now cutting sharply for the left corner of the end zone. Bobby's pass reached Danny's outstretched fingertips a split second before the fast-closing free safety arrived on the scene. Danny made sure his feet were in-bounds, and then pulled the leather ball into his chest as he hit pay dirt. Valley West led by a single point, 28 to 27. The snap on the extra-point try was bobbled, and by the time Rags McKenzie swung his foot he was engulfed with red-shirted West defenders. The scoreboard stayed Valley West 28, Rockland 27. There were just under four minutes remaining in the game.

On the sidelines, Coach Kirk considered attempting an onside kick, but with two of his three time-outs remaining, he decided against it. He chose instead to let his kickoff team try to pin Valley West deep in their own territory, and then let his defensive unit try to hold West's offense in check. His decision made sense, especially with Bo James firing up the defense for one final stand. However, the Valley West return man forgot to cooperate. He fielded the kickoff deep in his own territory, followed a wall of blockers up the middle, and then cut directly to his left. He outran two would-be tacklers and headed down the sidelines with only one man to beat. Rags McKenzie wasn't the fastest player on the kickoff team. He was, at best, an average tackler. And so, when the Rockland fans together with the entire Warrior bench saw that the only defender between the fleet-footed Valley West return man and the Rockland goal line was their kicker, a chorus of collective groans filled the air. At midfield, it looked as if Rags might have a shot to run down the ballcarrier. At the Rockland twenty-five it seemed that the West speedster was pulling away. And finally, at the Warrior five-yard line, Rags made a last-gasp effort to prevent disaster. He leaped at the flashing legs of the West return man. The contact he made was hardly more than a mini-bump, but it was enough to knock the ballcarrier off stride, and before he could regain his balance, he went out-of-bounds at the Warrior three-yard line.

It was first and goal for Valley West at the three, and three and a half minutes showed on the clock. On first down Bo James and Ross Tanner slammed the door on an attempted quick pitch, and the result was the loss of a yard. Rockland called its second time-out of the half. They had but one remaining. On second and goal from the four, Hank Harmon and Bubba Hinton refused to budge even an inch, and the result was no gain. Bo James elected to use Rockland's final timeout. With two minutes and fifty-seven seconds to go and no time-outs remaining, Valley West faced third and goal from the four. They decided to keep the ball on the ground. The Valley West coach decided that when in doubt, run your best play. Send your most reliable running back behind your best blocker. And so, West's big fullback led their vaunted off-tackle power play. For a second the Rockland line appeared to cave in. The tailback was at the two-yard line when he leaped for the end zone. He was airborne and heading for the end zone when Bo James met him with a hundred and ninety-five pounds of determined muscle. The two of them went down hard at the one. With no time-outs remaining, and the clock showing two minutes and thirty-eight seconds left, Valley West sent in their field goal unit. A field goal was as close as an extra point from here. The ball was positioned almost dead center. Three points would give West a four-point lead with only two minutes to play. Coach Kirk felt that his only chance was an all out blitz. On the snap of the ball, Bo James drove up the middle, raised both arms and took flight. If ever a player was in position to block a kick, Bo James was in position. Unfortunately, the holder, in this case the Valley West backup QB, had yanked the ball away and was rolling instead to his left. Ross Tanner flew into his face at the five-yard line, but the West quarterback simply lobbed the ball over the head of the desperate defender and his tight end pulled it in eight yards deep in the end zone. The score was now Valley West 34, Rockland 27. Now West set up to kick again. The kicker had been true all night. An extra point now would all but seal the West victory. The kicker struck the ball solidly, but not as solidly as Casey Michaels struck it a split second later. The result was a deflected extra point and the score remained Valley West 34, Rockland 27.

Coach Kirk now pulled out all the stops. He sent Bo James in to receive the kickoff. The Valley West coach had anticipated as much. West's kicker kicked a low squibber down the middle of the field. Rockland's Brian Hanlon returned it to his own thirty-three before being dumped by two West defenders.

The situation was desperate. With little more than a minute and a half remaining, Rockland needed to travel sixty-seven yards with no time-outs , and then make the extra point just to tie the game.

It wasn't impossible, but it certainly wasn't going to be easy. Not a fan in the stadium understood why Coach Kirk called for Bo James to run a sweep. Sure, he made nine yards, but he was tackled inbounds, and the clock continued to run. On second and one, Bo swept to the other side of the field. This time he went out-of-bounds after picking up twelve yards. The time left read fifty-seven seconds. The ball was marked at the Valley West forty-six-yard line. Perhaps, if Bo could continue to get out-of-bounds, the sweeps just might continue to work.

Danny hurried back to the huddle. Both the strong side safety and strong side linebacker were flying up to support the defensive ends. From the sidelines, Coach Kirk raised both of his hands, palms outstretched, and held them high over his head. He pointed to his right with his right index finger and then made a gesture of bringing his right hand hard behind his back. Bobby Williams nodded his head. The play had been designed for this situation. It was a gimmick play that counted on the other team over-pursuing to the side of the offensive flow. The two open palms indicated that the formation would be a double wing. The fingers spread wide indicated that both wing backs should split between five and seven yards, rather than their normal one to two. The backward gesture indicated that the play was to be a throwback pass. With it came the option for the player catching the throwback to either continue running or throw a second pass downfield to the end.

If everything went perfectly, it could mean a touchdown. Not everything did. The play started well enough. Bobby Williams threw the ball to his right wingback, who had taken three hard, driving steps forward, and then dropped back about five or six yards behind the line of scrimmage. He then threw directly across the field to Bo James, who would have both guards in front of him. He would then be given the option of running the ball or throwing it deep to either of the two ends, both of whom would be running their routes to Bo's side of the field.

The problem was that one of the Valley West linebackers had been assigned to cover Bo James at all times now. He was given the title of "monster man." Had he been mirroring the QB, he would have been said to be using a "spy" technique. At any rate, just as the wingback lofted the pass across the field toward Bo James, the monster linebacker charged to intercept the ball. Bo saw what was happening, and did his best to get between the ball and the linebacker. The ensuing collision could be heard throughout the stadium.

The play had been set up perfectly. Danny had been wide open at the five-yard line, but Bo hadn't been able to get to the football, and thus the play had failed. Time was running out, and Rockland was coming up short. When Danny returned to the huddle, Bo James jogged alongside of him. "Can you block Number 57?" Bo wanted to know.

"I think so," Danny said.

"Give it your best shot," said Bo.

Danny nodded. The Valley West coach must have seen Danny open on the play before. He assigned the tall, lanky safety to cover him all over the field, man-to-man. On the snap, Danny drove down across the middle of the field. His eyes were glued to Number 57. Bobby Williams took one step and fired the ball to Bo James out in the left flat. Both guards pulled to act as personal escorts. Danny banged into the big Valley West linebacker with his left shoulder. The blow spun him to the side, but it wasn't a solid block. The linebacker kept his eyes glued to Bo James. Perhaps that is why he never saw a tall, lanky

116

Valley West defender crash into him. Both of the defenders went down in a pile of arms, legs, and pads, and Bo James was on the loose. At the Valley West thirty, it looked as if excellent pursuit was going to save the day for West. They hadn't reckoned Bo James.

Bo stiff-armed the first defender; actually it was more like he bludgeoned him with his forearm. The defender went down like a pile of empty armor. Bo lowered his shoulder, and the second defender bounced off of him like an agate bouncing off a flipper in a pinball machine. The last defender was smallish, but super quick. He dove at Bo's legs in his best cross body block fashion. Bo high-stepped over his prostrate body into the Valley West end zone.

Just nine seconds remained on the scoreboard clock. This game, if Rags could convert the extra point, was heading for overtime.

Bo James never said a word. He didn't have to. Coach Kirk could see it in his face. He was spent. He had given every ounce of strength he had in him by going all out on both offense and defense. The plan had been to use him on offense only, but circumstances had required Coach Kirk to use Bo on both sides of the ball. Consequently, if the game went into overtime, Valley West would have the upper hand.

By nature, Coach Kirk was no gambler. Some might even call him conservative. He was, at the very least, cautious by nature. And so, when he raised his hand to indicate that Rockland would be attempting a two-point conversion, a murmur began in the Rockland stands. The "second-guessers" began buzzing among themselves. Of course, they had no way of knowing what Coach Kirk knew.

Coach Kirk never hesitated. He knew exactly what needed to be done, and he did it. He called the play he felt would give his squad their best chance to win the game and the championship.

The play began with Bo James going in motion from his left to his right. Every eye on the field watched the star as he moved away from the ball. Coach Kirk had counted on that being the case. On the snap, three defenders surrounded Bo James. It didn't matter. Bobby Williams turned and floated the ball to the opposite corner of the end zone. Only three people were prepared for the play. Bobby Williams was one of them. Danny Cannon was another, and a tall, lanky free safety who carried Valley West's hopes was the third.

As the ball floated for the far corner of the end zone, Danny went high into the air. The Valley West defender managed to get a few inches higher. Just as Danny reached for the ball, the taller free safety plucked it from above him. Danny Cannon realized he had been out-leaped, but as the two boys headed earthward, he refused to be out-fought. Summoning every bit of his strength, Danny grabbed as much of the football as he could get his hands on. The taller defender held on with all of his strength. The two landed in a tangle in the corner of the end zone. The nearest official had watched the struggle from only a few feet away, but even as he raced to the two struggling

118

warriors, he wasn't certain which of them had come up with the ball. In truth, even as the two athletes hit the earth, the struggle wasn't decided. The tall senior from Valley West had wanted the ball with every fiber of his body. He knew that if he held on to it, his team would win the championship. Danny Cannon, only a freshman, would have other opportunities to win a championship. Perhaps the Valley West player may have wanted the ball more than Danny. Perhaps he was physically a bit stronger. When fans get together many years after an event they may long speculate on "perhaps" and "what if," but when the referee untangled the two combatants, it was "The Kid Who Could" who had ripped the ball away and clutched the winning two-point conversion in his arms. Perhaps that is how legends get their start.

The Rockland fans exploded. The scoreboard flashed the score: Rockland 35-Valley West 34.

There were to be no further heroics. Rockland's Rags McKenzie placed the ball horizontally on the tee.

The only change Coach Kirk made was to substitute Bo James at safety in place of a sophomore linebacker who had been on the kickoff team. Bo's speed wasn't needed. The Rockland kickoff team contributed to the victory by smothering the return man at his thirty-seven-yard line.

No sooner had the loud and raucous horn blasted, signaling the end of the game, than jubilant Rockland fans streamed onto the field.

Moments later they had hoisted both Coach Kirk and Bo James upon their shoulders. Seconds later Danny Cannon joined them for the heroes' ride to the locker room.

Meanwhile in the stands, Steve Mitman hugged the mother of Rockland's youngest hero, and Red Evans beamingly informed everyone in earshot range "Number 88—that's my grandson, and he's wearing my old number."

Sometimes life is filled with happy endings.

DATE DUE
